D0962022

THE TURNING

FRANCINE PROSE
THE TURNING

HARPER TEEN
An Imprint of HarperCollinsPublishers

Library of Congress Cataloging-in-Publication Data is available.
ISBN 978-0-06-199966-6 (trade bdg.)

Typography by Erin Fitzsimmons
12 13 14 15 16   LP/RRDH   10 9 8 7 6 5 4 3 2 1
❖
First Edition

To Emilia and Malena

DEAR SOPHIE,

I'm afraid this is going to sound crazy. But a very strange thing just happened.

A huge seagull had been flying alongside the ferry ever since we left the dock. The seagull was escorting us, or really, escorting *me*, flying as fast as it had to, in order to stay right beside me, just beyond the railing. If I moved down the deck, it moved.

The morning was damp and misty, unusually cold for June. There were only a few passengers on deck, and they were wearing rain slickers with hoods that hid their faces and screened out this weird . . . relationship I was having with this bird.

It was so close I could have touched it, but I knew I wouldn't, and the bird knew it, too. I watched it for a few minutes, swooping on the updrafts and circling down again. Then I turned and watched the shoreline disappear, until I could no longer see my dad waving or my dad's truck. I looked out at the sea, into the chilly wet fog through which I kept trying to glimpse the islands, even though I knew they were too far away.

It was just at that moment that the bird turned its head and screamed.

I know: Screaming is what seagulls *do*. It's normal.

This one was screeching right in my ear. Anyone would have jumped—jumped right out of his skin. And yet it wasn't the noise or the loudness that startled me.

What made it creepy and scary was that the bird was screaming at me. Not at the boat but at me . . . it followed me as we moved. How nuts is that?

Okay, here comes the really crazy part. The screech was almost human. You're going to have to believe me, Sophie, when I tell you that I could understand what the bird was saying.

It screamed, "Jack! Don't do this! Turn around! Go home! Leave . . . leave . . . leave . . ." Its cry got softer and sadder as the bird veered away and flew off into the distance.

I told myself, Okay, dude. This is pretty cracked. The seagull is speaking English and calling you by name. You should go belowdecks for a while and chill and be around other people. What makes the whole thing even more confusing is that I'd been feeling okay. Maybe a little nervous—anyone would be—about leaving home for two months to go live on a tiny island in the middle of nowhere. But it's true what we kept telling each other, Sophie: two months isn't all that long. By August, I'll have earned at least part of the money I need to go to college. The same college as you. So when high school is over next year, we can *both* go, assuming we both get in. And somehow I feel sure we will. Two months is a long time to be away from you, but we'll be together again before the summer is over.

So I was kind of enjoying the ferry ride, the damp cool of the fog on my face, the salty sting of the sea. I was glad just to have a job, because this summer, as everyone knows, there *are* no summer jobs. Anywhere. This one was going to pay really well, and it sounded easy, though maybe a little boring. I wasn't feeling especially paranoid or anxious. So doesn't it seem strange to you that I imagined a seagull yelling at me to jump off the ferry and swim back to shore?

Boarding the ferry, I hadn't paid much attention to the other passengers. I'd been too busy struggling with my luggage. At the very last minute I'd thrown in more sneakers and boots than I'll probably ever need. My dad and I had wrestled with my duffel bag, and it had been a drama, finding a place to put it on the boat where no one would trip over it and it would be safe.

By the time we'd stowed it all away, the ferry whistle was blowing and my dad was saying I could still change my mind and come home. He said it made him uncomfortable, my going away to an island where there were no phones or internet or TV, so that we'd have to write letters, old-school, starting with *Dear* instead of *Hi!* And ending with *love* or *sincerely* instead of X's and O's.

I knew my dad felt guilty, because I had to get a job. The pizza place where I worked last summer went out of business. Lately my dad has hardly been getting any work, though he used to make good money building porches and additions, and renovating the kitchens and bathrooms of rich people's summer homes. But now, with the economic downturn, a lot of his former customers are deciding they could live with the kitchens and bathrooms they already had. And no one is building new houses, at least not in our town. If I want to go to college, which you know I do, I'm going to have to earn some of the money myself. I think it's made my dad feel like he failed, even though it's not his fault that half the country is out of work.

I told my dad that two months would pass in no time and that my job sounded like fun. There were supposed to be plenty of books in the house where

I would be staying, so I could read all kinds of stuff I hadn't had time for in school. I was bringing my laptop, with this portable printer he'd got me—the old-school kind you plug in to the computer—so I could write him plenty of letters. I could improve my writing skills, which would be helpful in college. I didn't feel I had to tell him I'd brought along my favorite video games, in case I got sick of reading and writing letters, which I knew I would.

The ferry whistle blew again. My dad and I hugged good-bye. And as the ship pulled away from the dock, I ran up on deck so he could see me waving. I was sad for a moment, but then the sadness passed, and I started to enjoy the ride. I don't know why I had that fantasy—or whatever it was—about the seagull.

I hadn't slept well the night before. Maybe I was just tired. I decided to go downstairs, which was set up like a big, friendly, warm café. I'd get a coffee with three sugars, chill out, and text you from the phone I'd brought along, even though I knew I wouldn't be able to use it on the island.

It turned out I couldn't text you. The message didn't go through. We were already too far from land. Really, it doesn't make sense. You can text from halfway around the world. Probably from the moon. But the minute we sailed toward the islands, we entered a major dead zone. I felt like I'd left the modern world behind and time-traveled back into the past. To tell you the truth, I was starting to feel a little stranded, marooned on the desert (I knew it wasn't a desert) island I hadn't even got to. I couldn't say I wasn't warned that, as far as modern technology is concerned, I could be spending the summer in the Neanderthal era. I just hadn't expected to leave the twenty-first century so soon.

Fortunately, I'd kept my laptop with me instead of packing it away in my duffel bag. I turned on my computer and started writing you this letter. I figured I might as well get a head start, get in practice for the summer. Last night, you kept reminding me that I'd promised to write you every day, though the boat that picks up and delivers the mail to the island comes only three times a week. I said I'd write a letter every night and save them, and send them to you in batches.

I got so involved in trying to tell you about the seagull that I sort of forgot where I was. When I looked up, an elderly couple was standing beside my table, asking if the empty seats were taken.

I told you I hadn't noticed the other passengers. But I'd noticed *them*, mainly because the guy was blind, and his wife held his arm and was constantly telling him, There's a step here, turn right, don't hit your head on the doorway. It was the wife who asked if they could sit with me. I couldn't exactly say no. The husband's milky eyes stared straight ahead, didn't blink, and saw nothing.

As I shut my laptop, the wife said she hoped they hadn't interrupted me. I'd seemed so intent on what I was doing. What had I been writing?

First I said, "Oh, nothing." Then I said, "A letter to my girlfriend."

The husband said, "We saw you having quite a time with that seagull up on deck. It would have scared the dickens out of *me*, a bird screaming at me like that."

Actually, it made me feel a little less crazy that the guy said he'd *seen* it. Though I couldn't help wondering how a blind man could have watched me and the bird having our one-sided conversation.

They asked me where I was going, and when I said Crackstone's Landing, the blind man and his wife turned toward each other. Even though he could no longer see, they hadn't lost the habit of exchanging meaningful glances. It made me wonder what it was about Crackstone's Landing that had gotten that reaction.

"Are you visiting?" asked the woman.

"Not exactly," I said. "I've got a summer job there. Looking after two kids."

"Odd," said the blind man. "Don't take this the wrong way, but don't people usually hire girls for jobs like that?"

"That's so old-fashioned and sexist, dear!" said his wife. "These days plenty of young men babysit and take care of children—"

I said, "They had a girl working there before me. But it didn't work out. She quit suddenly to get married. So they had to find someone quick. And I guess they thought that this time, since it was summer, they should hire a guy to play sports with the kids."

"No immediate wedding plans for you, I assume," the blind man said.

"No," I said.

"What do you know about the children you're going to take care of?" the lady asked me.

"Not much, except what their guardian, Mr. Crackstone, told me," I replied. I guess I could have told them more. I could have said there was no they who had hired me. There was only Jim Crackstone. But Mr. Crackstone was so obviously rich and powerful and intimidating, he seemed like more than one person. He'd seemed like a whole committee.

I thought about Jim Crackstone's law office, where I'd gone to meet him, and where he'd tried to put me at ease, but where I was totally *not* at ease even though he said I'd come highly recommended. I remembered staring at the art on Jim

Crackstone's walls—dozens of antique prints and paintings of exploding volcanoes. I'd wondered: What's up with that? What's the message there?

Jim Crackstone said he'd heard good things about me from his friend Caleb. Also known as Caleb Treadwell, also known as your father, Sophie. I could have told Jim Crackstone that every nice thing your dad said about me must be true, because your dad was hardly in the habit of saying nice things about me. But I wasn't sure that Mr. Crackstone would appreciate the joke. And I certainly wasn't going to say that all your dad really wanted was to put me on an island with an ocean between us for two months—two months during which I couldn't see you, not unless I quit and swam home.

Talking to the old couple, I remembered all sorts of details about my conversation with my new boss. Jim Crackstone wore a chunky gold ring in the shape of a dollar sign. Normally, I don't notice guy's clothes, but his suit, navy with a white pinstripe, was so amazing that I had to stop myself from reaching out to touch it. Mr. Crackstone asked me a few questions about my family. But I could tell he already knew that my mom had died of a stroke when I was six, and I lived with my dad, who never remarried. Not only did Jim Crackstone know all that but I could tell he'd made up his mind to hire me before I walked in the door.

So I wasn't all that surprised when he told me he was offering me a two-month job taking care of Flora and Miles, his niece and nephew. The boy was home for the summer from boarding school, to which he would return in the fall. And though they'd hired a full-time replacement teacher for the girl, who was being homeschooled until she was old enough to go away to study, her teacher wouldn't arrive until the end of August. Since it was the summer, Mr. Crackstone thought he would hire a young man, because of his recent disappointment with the children's previous teacher, who had left them in the lurch when her fiancé proposed. A young man could supervise the sports and games, the physical activity that the children badly needed, and also Jim Crackstone thought it might be good

for Miles to spend some time around a role model—
a young man who was a decent human being.

Something about the way Jim Crackstone's lip
curled when he said "decent human being" made
me think there was something he wasn't telling me.
It crossed my mind that there had been someone
who worked for him before who had definitely not
been a decent human being.

Mr. Crackstone explained that he was the children's legal guardian. Their parents, his brother and
sister-in-law, had been killed in a train wreck on
a trip to India when the children—now ten and
eight—were very young. He told me the children
lived with their longtime cook, Mrs. Gross. Their
house, the family home, was the only dwelling on
the island, not counting a few small cottages where
they'd put up the staff and guests, in the days
when they'd had a staff and guests. He told me there
was no internet or phone and, for the children's
benefit, no TV. He said that was his decision, because
he was determined to protect his niece and nephew
from the corrupting influences of modern society

and culture. For a moment, just for a moment, I almost said I couldn't do it. I like all those things— my phone and video games and TV—that I'd sort of taken for granted until I was faced with the prospect of living without them. Jim Crackstone must have noticed the dark look on my face. And that was when he told me how much he was willing to pay.

"Okay," I said. "Sounds good."

Then Jim Crackstone said, "Young man . . ." And I began to suspect that he'd already forgotten my name. "Young man, there's one more thing. And in a way it's more important to me than anything else we've discussed so far. And it's this: No matter what happens on the island, I don't want to know. Don't try to get in touch me with me, don't send me a letter or ask someone to reach me in any way. I'm a very busy man. I simply cannot be disturbed."

In a way, his saying this seemed unnecessary. He'd already told me the island had no phone or email. How did he think I would reach him and what did he imagine I would have to report? But the way he looked at me . . . once more it was like something else was being said *underneath* what he was saying. I had the feeling that he was threatening me, and that it had something to do with you, Sophie. That unless I promised and kept my promise, he'd tell your father on me, and your dad would tell you, and (even though I knew better) it would somehow make you think less of me, and we would break up. I'm not saying this makes sense. I'm just telling you what I was thinking.

"What if one of the kids gets sick or hurt?" I asked.

Jim Crackstone sighed. "Mrs. Gross will know how to deal with that."

"Okay," I told Jim Crackstone. "I get it. You won't see or hear from me until the two months are over. In case you want to debrief me or something—"

"Not even then," said Mr. Crackstone.

"All right," I said. "Not even then. You'll never see me again, if that's what you want."

He gave me my instructions and then I left him. I can't say I felt good after the meeting, but I had what seemed like an easy job for a lot of money. I wasn't going to complain.

I don't know why I'm putting this whole conversation in a letter to you. You already know it all, we talked about it so often before I left. Maybe I'm just writing it down because I didn't tell any of it to the blind man and his wife, and something about this job and my interview with Mr. Crackstone just keeps seeming so weird. I feel like if I talk about it enough—to you—maybe I'll figure something out.

Then I remembered the old woman had asked what I knew about the kids, so I said, "The children I'm going to be caring for are orphans. That's all I know."

"Oh dear," said the old woman. "That island has such a tragic history."

"Tragic how?" I asked.

"Well, to begin with," the husband said, "the first John Crackstone was among the pilgrims to die on the *Mayflower* expedition. He left a wife and two little children from whom the Crackstones are descended."

"And then there was that other story," said his

wife. "Very romantic and sad. By any chance have you read *Romeo and Juliet*?"

"Last year. In tenth grade," I said.

"One never knows," said the blind man. "What young people read these days. Anyway, sometime in the twenties, I believe, one of the Crackstone girls wanted to marry a local boy, and the family objected, and they eloped in a rowboat. Unfortunately, a storm came up, and swept them out to sea . . ."

His wife said, "They were never found."

It gave me a chill. Because it was sort of *our* story, Sophie, minus the rowboat and the death. Ha-ha. But your mom and dad definitely don't want us to be together. I'm not saying it's a family thing, like Romeo and Juliet, or that it's just because your family's rich and my dad works in construction. My dad would be more likely to renovate your dad's house than to ever go there for dinner. And your parents don't like that. If your dad can't separate us forever, he'll settle for the summer.

The blind man's wife said, "Wasn't there

something more recent, dear? Within the last few years? Another tragic incident connected with Crackstone's Landing? I seem to remember reading something in the papers, something unpleasant . . . I think someone died there, and there was some kind of police investigation . . ."

That got my attention. Someone died at this isolated place where I'm about to spend the next two months? There was an *investigation*?

"Do you know what happened? Who died?" I asked.

"I just can't recall," said the woman. "Can you, dear?"

"I can't either," the blind man said. Then he turned toward me. "But I'll tell you something, young fellow. I grew up two islands away, and from the time I was old enough to understand, I can remember people saying that Crackstone's Landing was haunted. That on foggy days you can see the ghosts of that couple who tried to escape in the twenties, in their little rowboat, bobbing around in the waves. It's ridiculous, what people choose to believe. Just to scare themselves."

His wife said, "But I wish I could remember what it was. That legal or criminal problem they had there, it was really quite recent . . ."

I didn't really want to hear any more, so I said, "It's been a pleasure meeting you. I think I need some air." It was true. The café was overheated, and an awful greasy smell was coming from the counter where they sold coffee and soggy doughnuts. And honestly, I didn't want to spend the whole trip talking to these two. . . . Something about them creeped me out, especially when all they could talk about was ghosts and death and tragedy at Crackstone's Landing. I really didn't need to hear that. It wasn't exactly calming me down.

The blind man said, "We understand. It's getting a bit rocky, isn't it? Fresh air is always the best thing to head off seasickness before it starts."

It was true what the blind man had said: the sea was getting choppy. I had to hold on to the railings as I went back upstairs. I felt a lot better out on deck, though the wind was wetter and colder than it had been before. But even the fog was refreshing after the choking-hot, steamy café.

The fog was so thick that I couldn't see very far into the distance . . . but I thought I saw something. A boat. Anyone would have been crazy to take such a small boat out in weather like this. Then the boat seemed to vanish—if it was ever there—and I thought of the blind man's story about the ghost boat appearing in the fog. I didn't know which would be worse—if the boat was carrying ghosts or living people, in danger. I wondered if I should tell someone, in case there were real people out there in trouble. The fog cleared for a moment, and I looked again. Nothing. Probably I'd imagined the boat. It sure couldn't have been a ghost boat. First, because there *are* no ghosts. And second, because we were still more than an hour from Crackstone's Landing, and that little ghost boat would have had to cover a very long distance.

I was trying to pump myself up. Get my nerve back. Obviously, I wasn't wild about hearing creepy stories about the island where I was going, isolated from everything and everyone I knew, separated from the real world for two entire months. I didn't know what was wrong with me . . . first the stupid seagull fantasy and then I thought I was seeing ghosts. Maybe I was just missing you, Sophie. Maybe I was just trying to come up with excuses to turn around and come home.

I pulled my hoodie over my head. It had begun raining, lightly but still sharp and cold, like a shower of tiny ice needles. Now there was only one other person on deck. A woman in a summer dress, not warm enough for the weather at all. She was very thin and had long red hair. She stood against the railing, staring at the sea.

I can practically hear what you're thinking, Sophie. Maybe it's because we're so close, but a lot of times it's almost like I can hear your voice in my head and I know what you would say and how you would respond to what's happening. I know you're probably thinking that the redheaded girl was pretty. Not that you're a jealous person. Why would you be jealous when I haven't looked at another girl since I met you?

But she was pretty. I saw that when she turned. She would have been really pretty if her eyes weren't red-rimmed and swollen from crying. I couldn't quite tell how old she was. Early twenties, I guess. And something about her scared me. She looked not just unhappy but way *beyond* unhappy. I don't know why, but I suddenly thought, Damn! She's going to jump!

Great, I thought. This is really great. I haven't been gone an hour. Already a seagull freaks me out, a blind man tells me that the place I'm going is haunted or cursed or whatever, and I see a girl about to dive off the side of the boat. These are not good signs! Maybe something's trying to send me a message, and I should listen to that seagull. I should have gone for it when my dad said there was still time to change my mind.

I crept up closer to the woman and calculated how fast I would have to move to drag her back if it really started to look as if she was about to go over the side. She was so thin and delicate, she couldn't be very strong. Even if she was struggling, I could take her down with one arm.

Imagine how relieved I was when she just turned and walked away from the edge of the deck. She brushed past me without looking at me, as if I wasn't there. Rubbing her arms—she was shivering—she went down to the café.

I stayed on deck for a while. Then I thought what a drag it would be if I showed up on the island sick. Hi, I'm the new babysitter, and I'm here to give your kids the flu!

So I went downstairs again. The blind man's wife waved to me, but I pretended not to notice and kept walking.

More of the tables were occupied. Where had all these passengers come from? Maybe they were all ghosts. Joke. For the first time, I looked around to see who was traveling with me. And for a moment I envied them, the men and women and kids on vacation, on their way to the summer home or the big family reunion, the cousins all playing touch football, the barbecues and parties on the lawn. It was a life I knew only from movies—until I met you and we went to your aunt's party on the lawn, and everyone was playing touch football.

I envied them. I did. My easy, high-paying summer job was already starting to seem like a two-month jail sentence on some cursed (and haunted!) prison island.

Then I saw the redheaded girl again. She was sitting at a table and playing cards with a much older man, a guy with black eyebrows and thick silver hair, older-guy movie-star handsome. He'd given her his jacket, and she no longer looked cold. I could tell that the guy was winning. And suddenly I knew that the reason the woman had been crying had something to do with losing the game, with how much or what she was losing. I can't tell you why I was so sure, but I promise you I knew: they were playing for big stakes—bigger than money—and the redheaded girl was losing.

I kept trying to look away. But no matter where I tried to look, I'd find myself staring at them. They were so involved in their game, they didn't know anyone else was there. But you know how some-times you can feel you're being watched even when you don't see anyone watching? The guy must have sensed my interest because he looked up from the cards and turned and stared straight at me.

His eyes were black and opaque, like two dark marbles. Where had I just seen eyes like that before?

Then I remembered: the seagull.

I *really* needed to chill out. Okay, I didn't want to go away for the summer, but this was ridiculous. I powered on my laptop. I went back to writing this letter to you.

I don't know how much time passed before the ship's conductor found me and told me that we'd be docking at Crackstone's Landing in twenty minutes.

For a moment I wondered why I was getting special treatment, why he wasn't telling anyone else that their stop was coming up. And then I remembered that I would be the only passenger getting off at that stop.

I guess I'd better shut this down and get my

luggage and get ready to leave the boat. I'll write you again from the island.

Keep the faith. Write me. Meanwhile,

Love you,

Jack

THE DARK HOUSE
CRACKSTONE'S LANDING
JUNE 2

DEAR SOPHIE,

I guess I must be more superstitious than I'd thought. I'd been seeing bad omens the whole time on the ferry. But as we neared the island, the signs suddenly got better.

First, the weather cleared dramatically. The sun burned through the fog, and the island appeared, emerald green, shimmering in the light. From far away, I could see a willow dipping its leaves in the water. I'd never seen a tree growing so near the sea. A long white beach took up part of the shore, hedged by a stone embankment. The whole island looked like a garden, lawns and fields rising to a low hill, on which I could just make out the roof and chimneys of an enormous house surrounded by tall pointed trees.

The next good sign was the brand-new red pickup truck parked at the end of the dock. I don't know what I'd imagined, exactly. Maybe I'd been thinking that someone from the house would come to pick me up in a horse-drawn buggy.

The minute I set foot on the dock, a woman jumped out of the truck. She was around your mom's age, the age my mother would have been, but kind of tough and muscular, and she moved like someone much younger. She was wearing jeans and a plaid shirt, a tan jacket, and hiking boots that, on her, looked cool and stylish.

Mr. Crackstone had told me the kids lived alone with their cook, a widow named Mrs. Gross. I guess it was pretty stupid of me to have pictured a fat, unpleasant-looking woman whose appearance matched her name.

The woman held out her hand, and I shook it.

Her palm was calloused and rough.

"Linda Gross," she said. "Call me Linda."

"Good to meet you, Linda. I'm Jackson Branch. Call me Jack."

"Welcome to Crackstone's Landing, Jack," Linda said. "I'd imagined someone different."

I wondered what she'd expected. Someone older and more grown-up? Someone better dressed? Some brawny physical-trainer type weighed down by sports equipment?

I said, "I did, too."

"I don't want to know what you imagined," said Linda. "Hey, look. You made the drizzle stop! It was cold and nasty this morning."

By now two crew members had got off the boat and were unloading cartons of stuff for the house and putting them in the back of Linda's truck.

"Hiya, Linda," they said. "No mail today. Any letters going out?"

"Just a couple of bills," said Linda, handing one of the guys a few business envelopes.

"When aren't there bills?" he said.

"You can say that again," said Linda. "Good thing I'm not actually the one paying them." The workers kept on going back and forth from the boat to the truck. It was amazing how many boxes they were delivering.

"Thanks, guys, as always," said Linda.

"It's crazy," she told me. "I have a little garden that's just started producing peas and lettuce. But except for that, and for the rest of the year, everything has to be shipped in. *Everything.* Paper towels, clothes for the kids, grass seed for the gardeners. Like I said, I'm glad I'm not paying the bills."

Standing there talking to Linda, I'd almost forgotten for a moment where I was and how I'd gotten there and what I was doing. It was almost as if we were old friends meeting on the street. But the minute she mentioned the fact that everything came in by ferry, I remembered: no internet, no phone. And it crossed my mind that, as far as Jim Crackstone was concerned, I was just another bit of cargo off-loaded from the boat and delivered to the island.

Linda was waiting for me to answer a question I hadn't heard.

"Excuse me?" I said.

"I was asking if you smoked," said Linda.

"I don't," I said.

"Good. I don't, either," said Linda. "No one should. But every so often I indulge. Do you mind?"

"No," I said. "My dad smokes."

"Good," said Linda, lighting up. "Believe me, I would never ever smoke in the house."

"I believe you," I said.

"How was the ferry ride?" asked Linda.

"Fine," I said. "Uneventful. A little choppy at the end." No way I was going to tell her that I'd met a seagull that warned me to turn around and not go to the island—the same island on which an obviously nice person had come to pick me up in an obviously nice red truck. Maybe after a few weeks, I could mention to Linda that on my way here this unnerving event had happened, or I *thought* it happened. Even now the seagull seemed less real by the minute. Maybe Linda and I would laugh about my hallucination on the ferry. Eventually I would tell her how the blind man's wife had mentioned something about a . . . problem and an investigation. But I couldn't exactly say, Hi, nice to meet you, is it true that someone died here and the cops were involved?

The blast of the ferry horn startled me. Even Linda flinched. But the men unloading the cartons yelled, "Okay! Shut up! We're coming!" I couldn't stop staring at how full they'd packed Linda's truck. Groceries, I got that. People needed to eat. But how much could Linda, the two kids, and I possibly consume? Toilet paper, paper towels. Shampoo, lightbulbs, toothpaste. I saw a large box labeled with the name of the high-tech vacuum cleaner that the know-it-all British guy advertises on TV.

At last the men got back in the boat, the walkway came up, and the ferry began to pull away from shore. I looked up at the deck.

The sad-looking red-haired woman was gazing over the railing. For a few moments I was sure that she was looking at me. But she was already too far away for me to be sure. She was definitely too far away for me to see if she was still crying. I wondered who had won that card game. I couldn't stop myself from waving. She didn't wave back. She probably didn't even see me.

"Friend of yours?" said Linda.

For a moment I longed to tell Linda about how sure I was, without knowing why, that the woman had been thinking about jumping off the boat. And about how I was certain that she and the guy in the café had been playing cards for something that she couldn't afford to lose. But I didn't know Linda well enough, and I didn't want her first impression to be that I was some kind of crazy kid, or someone who made everything into a drama just to get attention. I shook my head in answer to her question.

"Let's go," said Linda. "I know the kids are waiting. They're excited to meet you."

I said, "Two kids alone in the house? They're probably tearing the place apart."

Linda gave me a funny look. "Not these kids," she said.

I wanted to ask what she meant. But I couldn't think how to put the question so she wouldn't think I was being nosy or trying to make her say more than she wanted to.

The cab of Linda's truck smelled loamy and good, like the earth after a rain. She drove quickly and confidently, sort of like my dad.

I said, "How long you have you lived here?"

Linda said, "I moved here when the children did. They were practically babies. I'd been the cook for their family. The kids' dad, rest in peace, found me working in a local diner and hired me on the spot. The kids' parents were really great. And when they . . ." Her voice trailed off. "I was married then. My husband came with us when we all moved here and worked as the handyman on the island, but he got sick and died two years ago. Sometimes it seems like yesterday and sometimes like a million years ago."

"I'm sorry," I said. I was about to bring up how my mom died when I was little. But I sensed that it would only make the mood in the truck turn darker.

Later there would be time to tell Linda all about it, if I felt like it. Meanwhile I was already wishing that my dad could meet someone like Linda. Maybe I could introduce them after the summer was over.

"When we first came to the island," Linda said, "there was a nurse and a nanny and a gardener. There have been others since. People have come and gone. People who had a lot more influence over the kids than I did. If the kids seem a little . . . odd to you, I can't take any blame or credit. Maybe they were born that way. The mom was royalty, supposedly, but she was always really nice to me and never acted superior or snooty. Some of the teachers the kids have had . . ." Linda shook her head. "Well! I suppose they're unusual children, not that I remember anymore what *usual* children are. But I have nieces and nephews I see sometimes, and trust me, they're not like Miles and Flora."

"What are Miles and Flora like?" I said.

"Sometimes I almost feel like they're from another era completely," Linda said. "But you'll see what I mean. Anyway, the entire Crackstone's Landing population is down to us three. Me and the kids. And now here you are, bringing the total to four."

The dirt road led through a field in which tall grasses and wildflowers grew thickly on each side.

"Awesome field," I said. It took all my self-control not to ask what she meant by calling the kids a "little odd."

Linda seemed not to hear me. "It's not a life for everyone. Most people would get lonely, I guess. Freaked out by the solitude and the silence. But I've always liked it. I grew up in the country."

We crossed the field and drove through a patch of woods so neat that the forest floor seemed to have been swept clean. Then we came into a clearing, through a stone gate, and past a series of gardens, like walled, flowered rooms leading off the corridor of the road.

I said, "Do you do all this yourself?"

"Are you kidding? Hank Swopes, the landscape guy, comes once a week, with a crew. He has his own boat. He's kind of cranky, but if you're nice to him, he'll sometimes mail a letter for you or bring you back something special from the mainland. We used to have a full-time gardener. Did I say that? I can't remember. But he's not with us anymore. It didn't work out."

A tightness in Linda's voice made me think that maybe the full-time gardener had been a boyfriend or something. Maybe after her husband died. Or anyway, someone special.

"Here we are," she said. "The Dark House."

Towers and gables and peaked roofs rose from the huge wooden structure. There were porches and windows and a slanted roof in which there were windows suggesting attics, and attics on top of attics. And all of it, including the trim, was painted a deep coal black that seemed to swallow up all the light.

I felt the hairs on my neck and arms rise. The house seemed like some hulking black monster or a dark hole you could fall into when you walked through the door.

Linda didn't seem to notice my reaction. She said, "Strange color choice, I know. But it's been like that for so long . . . decades and decades and decades.

And every time it's repainted, it stays black. It's written, almost like a law, in some family papers. I know most people think it's creepy, but you'll come to love it, I promise. It's . . . unusual, like the kids. Though two months may not be long enough for you to see how perfect it is. It just wouldn't look *right* if the house was white or gray. Yellow would be ridiculous, and what other colors are there, really?"

"Serious Goth," I said. "Before its time." What else could I say?

"I guess you could say that," said Linda. "Or maybe after its time. The tradition started when that poor unfortunate couple drowned all the way back in the twenties."

I said, "I heard about that from these old people I met on the boat." Probably this would have been a good moment to ask about that more recent thing that happened, the "incident" that the blind man's wife couldn't remember. But I couldn't think of how to begin, and I didn't want to interrupt Linda.

"After they were lost at sea, the girl's father,

the snobby idiot who'd forbidden them to marry, which is why they'd eloped in the first place, was so grief-stricken and guilty he ordered the house to be painted black, and for it to stay that color forever. It's been repainted twice since I've been here. I don't even have to explain to the painters that it's what Mr. Crackstone wants. Everybody knows about this place. It makes things kind of easy and, in another way, kind of hard. I guess the house doesn't look very welcoming, does it? Oh, well. I'm going to pull the truck around to the back so we can bring all this stuff directly into the kitchen, if you don't mind. It's not the most formal way to introduce you to the house, but—"

"I don't mind," I said.

Linda drove around the house, which was larger than it looked from a distance and more complicated and elaborate. Strange additions jutted out from unexpected places. There were porches, walkways, covered verandas, bay windows, a hexagonal tower attached to one corner, and several more towers you couldn't see from the front. It certainly looked like a haunted house. But I already knew that, if I asked, Linda would tell me it was just a house painted black. Unusual, but still just a house. Hey, I told myself, it's only a house.

I said, "This old blind man on the boat told me people sometimes saw ghosts of the couple who drowned." I laughed, but it sounded fake.

Linda gave me a searching look. She said, "It seems like people on that boat had a lot to say about us." Then she burst out laughing. "Years ago I read this story in the papers about a British castle whose owners needed money, so they opened the place to tourists and overnight guests and tried to drum up business by claiming the house was haunted by the ghosts of some English queen. They offered special vacation packages on Halloween, or whatever they call it in England. Paint your house an unusual color, and you won't believe the stories people come up with. The stuff people say. If you're even a little different, or you live by yourself, people make up all kinds of things. Don't believe everything you hear. Let's go."

I wondered what it meant, or if it meant anything at all, that Linda used the world *unusual* so often. Maybe she was nervous about how I'd react to the house and the kids, and she was trying to prepare me. But I couldn't give it much thought, because I was too busy loading my arms with boxes to carry into the kitchen.

I heard Linda say, "Oh, look, here's Miles and Flora."

I turned and saw the children watching me from the doorway . . .

I'll write again tonight, I promise. I think I need a whole letter to tell you what they were like.

Until then, stay strong. Stay chill. Write to me now!

Love, Jack

CRACKSTONE'S LANDING

JUNE 2

DEAR DAD,

Just a note to say I got here okay, and everything's fine. The kids are cool, and the cook is named

Linda. You'd like her a lot. The summer's going to be easy and fun. I'll be home in no time. I'll write more when I get a chance.

Love you,

Jack

THE DARK HOUSE
JUNE 2

DEAR SOPHIE,

There's a lot I could say about Miles and Flora. Number one, they're very quiet. Reserved, as if they're watching to see who you are—who I am—before they reveal the slightest thing about themselves. And they're polite, like miniature grown-ups. Miniature, polite grown-ups. Now I know why Linda looked at me strangely when I joked that the kids might tear the house apart when she was gone. If these kids track mud on the floor, they run to clean it up.

But the first thing I noticed, the first thing anyone would notice, was that they looked like little fashion models—like little fashion models from another planet. Like angels or creatures from a parallel universe where everyone is perfect. They both have enormous black eyes, bright and round and startled, like the eyes of the nocturnal creatures that sometimes appeared on the road, frozen in the beams of my dad's headlights.

Miles has bright red hair (of course I thought of that unhappy woman on the ferry), and Flora has long black curls all the way down her back. For some reason I'd expected them to look pale, as if they spent all their time indoors, but they actually looked healthy, like they went out a lot. They certainly don't look like regular American kids. You kind of get the feeling they've just landed from somewhere else and haven't yet completely decided if they want to stay. I remembered their mom was from India. Maybe that explained it.

Linda said, "Miles and Flora, this is Jack."

Just because I don't have siblings doesn't mean I've never been around kids. I know kids usually ignore you, either because they're shy or because adults or older kids don't interest them all that much. Usually kids stand there staring at the ground, basically just waiting for you to lose interest and go away. But Miles and Flora looked me straight in the eye, then stepped forward and shook my hand (first Miles, then Flora).

"Hey, kids," I said. "What's up?"

"We're very well, thank you," said Flora. "And you?"

What was it Linda said about them? From another era. They weren't even dressed for this century. Flora wore a long white gown, edged with lace. And Miles wore pants, a blazer jacket with a crest on the pocket, and—you're not going to believe this— a tie. I assumed he'd put on his boarding-school uniform. Had they dressed up especially to meet me? Or did they dress like that every day? There was starting to be a long list of things I wanted to ask Linda. *Unusual* was the word, all right.

I could see that I had my work cut out for me. Not that the kids would be any trouble. Discipline would not be an issue. But whatever Jim Crackstone had hired me to do, it occurred to me that my real job would be to spend the summer teaching them to be normal kids. I was a little surprised, because Linda was so relaxed and warm, and the kids she'd taken care of practically since birth were so formal and chilly. But she'd said they'd had other teachers. I wondered who had taught them to act like someone's uptight parents.

Then we just stood awkwardly shifting from foot to foot. You know me, I'm not exactly the quietest person on the planet. But suddenly I couldn't think of anything to say. What's your favorite TV show? What music do you like? How do you like school? They didn't watch TV, and Flora didn't go to school.

Maybe I should have asked them how a normal kid kept from going crazy with nothing to do on this island, but I figured I'd find out soon enough. And the truth was . . . well, they almost scared me a little. I felt like I'd have to get to know them a lot better before I could ask them even slightly personal questions.

"Can we help you, Linda?" said Miles. At least he called her Linda and not Mrs. Gross.

Linda said, "Kids, take those grocery bags inside. Jack, can you get that vacuum? Right, that big box there. And I'll grab these paper towels and stuff."

The kitchen was bright and cheerful, with windows on three sides and the sunlight beaming directly on an old-fashioned enamel stove. Linda flicked a glass crystal hanging in one window, and a scatter of bright rainbows danced over the appliances, the shiny pots and pans, the shelves of dishes, and the pale green walls. For a moment I kind of missed my dad. I was thinking about how he'd always tried to make sure our kitchen was welcoming and neat, and how after Mom died he taught himself to cook my favorite foods. Maybe I could teach Linda how to make my dad's special meatballs and spaghetti. Sugar in the tomato sauce. Just a pinch, like he'd showed me.

"Are you hungry?" said Linda. "You must be starved."

"I am a little," I said.

"Okay," said Linda. "Hold everything!" Miles and Flora watched Linda slap together a thick sandwich of delicious ham and cheese with lettuce and the perfect amount of mayonnaise. Then the kids watched me scarf it down in about fifteen seconds. I felt like I was a tiger or a seal they were watching get fed at the zoo.

"Aren't you hungry?" I asked them.

"No thank you," Miles said. "We had a very delicious lunch."

These kids were definitely not like any kids I knew.

When we'd unloaded the last package and I'd got my duffel bag and luggage and backpack from the truck, Linda said, "Miles and Flora, why don't you take Jack upstairs and show him his room?"

I picked up the duffel bag and told Linda I'd get the rest later. Miles grabbed my backpack, and though it was half as big as he was, I let him carry it. Let him feel like a big boy in his little jacket and tie.

"Take the flashlight," said Linda.

"The flashlight?" I said. It was late afternoon, but there was still plenty of daylight.

Linda shrugged. "Some of the halls are pretty dark, and I can't always keep on top of when the lightbulbs burn out. Plus I always have to stop the kids from closing the curtains. For some mysterious reason they seem to like it dark. Don't you, kids?"

Miles and Flora looked at each other.

"We don't need the flashlight," said Miles.

Linda said, "I know you guys can find your way around in the dark, like baby raccoons. But it might be harder for Jack—"

"We can help him," said Miles.

"Hey, I'll be fine," I said lamely. I'd come there to take care of the kids, and already everyone was acting like I was the one who needed help. I had to take charge. Jim Crackstone hadn't hired me so the kids could take care of me.

"Follow us," said Flora, and skipped on ahead of her brother. I don't know why I needed reassurance, exactly, but it reassured me to walk behind Miles, so that I was walking behind my own backpack. Inside it, I knew, were the video games I would teach the kids when things got slow, and I was beginning to think they would get pretty slow, pretty soon. I especially liked knowing that inside the pack was my laptop. I could write letters to you. It made me feel like you were a little less far away. I heard your voice inside my head, saying, "Only two months!"

But two months had already begun to seem like an eternity. Maybe anyone would have felt edgy, heading into a dark, spooky house where he was going to spend the summer. Anyone would have felt jumpy leaving the comfortable kitchen, where Linda was putting away paper towels, a normal thing that normal people did in any normal household. I felt like I did when my dad and I went to the amusement park for my birthday, when I was eight. Following Miles and Flora, I felt those stomach flutters like when they belt you in for the haunted house ride, and the car starts rumbling along the track, and all you can think about is how soon you'll enter the dark tunnel and the ghosts and monsters will start popping out of the walls.

What made me feel even worse was that it seemed as if all the light had decided to stay behind in the kitchen. A thick velvet curtain covered the door that led to the rest of the house, and when it swung shut behind us, I went semiblind for a minute until my eyes adjusted. Miles and Flora ran ahead. They certainly did seem to know their way in the dark. Maybe it didn't seem dark to them, and maybe soon it wouldn't seem dark to me, once I got used to it. I reminded myself how places and people look different, once you get to know them. Remember how, when we first met in the school lunchroom, I thought you were stuck-up and snobby and you thought I was a weirdo nonstop talker?

The halls weren't exactly pitch-black, but they were pretty dim. All the windows were covered by heavy curtains. The lamps that worked were so low-wattage they could have been candles. And nothing was laid out the way you'd expect. Wouldn't you think that a hall would eventually lead to a room? But some halls led only to other halls that right-angled and doubled back. We went up a winding staircase and down a corridor, then up a staircase, across a sort of bridge, and down another staircase. I couldn't tell how far we'd come or what floor we were on or if the kids were messing with my head by taking me the long way. We passed a lot of doors that were closed and looked as if they hadn't been opened in a long time. Maybe they were locked. Miles and Flora weren't exactly giving me the guided tour of all the interesting parts of the house we passed on the way to my room.

I felt as if Miles and Flora were the grown-ups, and I was the child, being led through the maze to the center of the labyrinth, where the witch or monster waited. I thought, You should be dropping bread crumbs or M&M's or any of the secret markers that smart children in fairy tales use when they're being led into the forest and they want to find their way home. But Miles and Flora knew exactly where they were going, and all I had to do was follow. Still, my duffel bag was getting heavier by the minute, and I could only imagine how heavy my backpack was beginning to seem to little Miles.

"We're almost there," Miles said.

Suddenly the corridor dead-ended at a door. This one was definitely locked. Miles tried to open it, then Flora, and then I turned the knob and even banged on the door, though I knew it was stupid. There was no one behind it. I hoped.

"What's up with this?" I asked them. "What's inside the room?"

The kids exchanged another one of those looks I'd seen pass between them in the kitchen.

"Don't worry," Flora told me. "There are other ways. We can go around."

I said, "Whoever designed this place must have been pretty twisted."

Miles said, "It happened over a long time. Our great-great-grandparents and then my great-grand-parents kept building new additions and firing and hiring architects, so the floor plan got kind of scrambled."

"Why did they hire and fire so many?" I said.

"I thought the architects all quit!" said Flora.

"You heard wrong," Miles said quietly. "You often do."

Flora was silent after that.

I told myself, You just got here. It's too early to tell the kid to talk nicer to his sister.

Anyhow, I was starting to understand that the children had secrets. Their quick, silent glances were like a private language invented to keep strangers—like me—from finding out what they didn't want me to know. Already I sensed that the secrets they shared were part of why they seemed so strange, and were about something more serious than whether the architects who'd built their house had been fired or quit. The big, dark house was their world, and they were letting me in. But only so far.

We passed a dusty living room, where I could tell that no one ever sat on the dusty velvet couches and no one ever built a fire in the huge stone fireplace. At least not for a very long time. Finally we came to a large room in which a row of chairs ringed the mirrored walls. In the middle of the floor was a gigantic pool table. I was practically ecstatic.

I said, "You guys play pool?"

A giant cobweb covered half the table, and as the pale light from doorway trickled in, I thought I saw something disgusting scurry through the furry webbing. But that was easily fixable. Hadn't Linda just bought a brand-new vacuum cleaner? Flip the switch and the tarantula nest would be toast in thirty seconds.

This time Miles and Flora looked up at me as if I'd asked if they liked to eat the spiders that lived on the pool table.

Miles said, "I guess somebody must have played, once. But we don't . . ."

I said, "Would you like to learn?"

"I'm not very good at sports," said Flora.

"I bet we could find a pool cue your size."

Miles and Flora exchanged a whole new set of solemn, secretive looks.

I wanted to say, Come on, kids. You can trust me. I promise. But I told myself, Shut up. If I said too much too soon, I would only alarm them. And if I scared them now, I could give up on the rest of the summer.

Relax, I told myself. You've been here fifteen minutes. You weren't going to be best friends right away. . . . Of course the kids are a little shy—orphaned when they were tiny, growing up in a creepy old mansion on a deserted island. That was enough to make anyone "unusual," especially children whose only living relative is paying good money so he won't have to see them or hear one word about them. And whatever Miles learned in school about the outside world, he seemed to have forgotten it all when he returned to the island.

We backed out of the billiards room and headed down another hall, then up another flight of stairs so steep and narrow it reminded me of the staircase on the ferry, though it was a lot easier to get up the stairs when the floor wasn't being rocked and pitched around by the ocean.

"Where are *your* rooms?" I said.

Miles said, "Oh, pretty far away. On the other

side of the house."

I'm afraid this is going to sound crazy.

But when the kids said that, I had this insane thought that the children were little vampires, and that every night they went back to their tombs somewhere in the basement. Remember we saw that vampire film that everyone loved, and we kind of enjoyed it but agreed it was silly? I know they're just lonely little kids who have no friends and never learned from other kids what normal kids are supposed to act like. I wish that you were here with me, Sophie. You'd know how to talk to them; you're the oldest in your family. You had all that practice with your two sisters, your little brother, and then the twins.

I said, "Tell me something, kids. Am I going to be able to find my way around here? Or am I constantly going to get lost without you two leading me around?"

Miles said, "Maybe you'll get lost once or twice. But you'll figure it out. They always do."

"They?" I said.

"Visitors," Flora said quickly.

"I didn't know you kids got all that many visitors," I said, instantly sorry. I didn't want them to think I was saying they didn't have any friends, which they obviously didn't.

"You're a visitor," said Miles.

"I'll be here for two months," I said.

"That's a long visit," said Flora.

Finally, Miles opened a door to a huge attic with skylights, armchairs, rugs, a bed, a desk. On the bed was a striped blanket, and on the wall were paintings in simple wooden frames. The room was spacious and bright and smelled new, like wood shavings. Actually, it smelled like my dad when he came home from a carpentry job.

"This is your room," Flora said.

Miles said, "If you like it."

"Are you kidding?" I said. "It's awesome."

"Linda fixed it up just for you," Flora said.

"So no one lived here before?" I said.

"No," said Miles, and Flora said, "No," almost at the same moment, and for the first time I was pretty sure they were telling the truth and not trying to keep something secret.

I liked the idea of a room created just for me, because . . . I promise, this is my last crazy thought of the day. For some reason it crossed my mind that if the house was really haunted, it would take the ghosts longer to find me in a room that no one had lived in before. Maybe by the time the ghosts figured out I was there, two months would be over, and it would be time to leave the island. Are you laughing at me, Sophie? I hope so!

I sensed that Flora wanted to hang around and watch me unpack. But Miles said, "We'll be leaving now if you think you'll be okay without us."

I said, "I'll be fine, thanks, kids. I'll see you soon." I looked at my watch. It was almost four. "Maybe I'll take a nap. Don't let me sleep through dinner, okay?"

"Should we come get you?" said Flora.

I said, "I can find my way back." It would have seemed too pathetic to ask the kids to come help me and keep me from getting lost inside their own house. I was supposed to be in charge. "Just tell Linda to make sure to call me."

Miles said, "We will, but I don't know how well you can hear anyone from here."

The kids exchanged one more look. This one gave me the chills. Then it was over so fast I wasn't even sure I'd seen it.

"We'll tell Linda," Flora said. They turned around and left.

Don't get me wrong, Sophie. I like the kids, sort of. They're interesting. That's for sure. Still, it felt good to be alone and have a few hours to rest in my room, which was a million times nicer and more spacious than anything I'd imagined. Though now, come to think of it, I had no idea what I'd imagined.

I set my laptop up on the wooden desk, beside a window. From my chair I can see beautiful gardens with hedges and flower beds rolling down to a huge lake. A little rowboat is bobbing in the water beside a dock. Down to my right is a tennis court and, nearby, a volleyball net. I can deal with this! The place is like a resort! A private room, a lake, a tennis court, and all I have to do is play with two eccentric kids. And I'm going to get paid for it. Two hundred dollars a week!

I had my own closet, nestled under the eaves of the pointed roof. It had been swept out, and inside there were hangers and a small chest of drawers. I lined up the ridiculous number of sneakers and shoes I'd brought, in a neat row. I hung up my hoodies and folded away my socks and jeans and T-shirts. I knew that no one would go through my things, but still, I don't know why—paranoid, I guess—I put my video games underneath my shirts and socks.

I was feeling chill, pretty squared away, and I sat down at the desk and wrote most of this letter to you. There was so much I had to say. After a while I got up and looked around the room. Most of the paintings on the walls were of the island or the sea. One painting was of the Dark House before it went dark. The house was a pale pigeon gray, but it still looked creepy. The sky behind it was blue, and you could tell that the artist had really tried his best to make the place seem cheerful, but it still looked like a haunted house.

Jim Crackstone had made quite a big deal about how many books they had in the house. But I hadn't noticed any on my way here. So obviously, there were parts of the huge house that I hadn't yet seen. Anyhow, there are books in my room. Two long shelves line one wall. I have to kneel down to read the titles. Nearly all of the volumes are old, and many are slightly dusty. Maybe dusting the books was what killed off Linda's old vacuum cleaner. There are books about geography and old-fashioned adventure books for kids, books about the Roman Empire, novels, gardening books. I didn't think they'd been chosen especially for me. I picture Linda scooping up armfuls of random books and bringing them up to my room. Like more furniture, in a way.

I ran my finger along the spines of the books until one of them stopped me. That was actually how it felt, as if the book exerted a force that magnetically pulled my hand toward it. It was newer than the rest of the books, though the design was supposed to look vintage. It had an odd shape, thinner and narrower than a normal book. The cover was pale yellow cloth, stenciled with a bouquet of roses and, for some reason, a lighthouse.

The title was *Great Love Poems*. I opened it to the first page. Someone had written an inscription in brown ink, in old-fashioned calligraphy with thick letters and lots of curlicues.

From Romeo to Juliet. With all my love.

I thought of the blind man and his wife. That's what they'd called the couple who'd tried to escape and drowned. Romeo and Juliet. Linda had mentioned them, too. They'd all said that the drowning had happened in the 1920s.

I looked to see when the poetry book had been published.

1989.

Well, I suppose there must have been more than one Romeo and Juliet on Crackstone's Landing. Probably every couple thinks of themselves that way, especially when their parents aren't exactly crazy about the idea of their being together. Like you and me, Sophie.

Maybe some guy who stayed in the house for a while gave the book to his wife for her birthday and was trying to be all corny and romantic. I guess it didn't work out all that well if Juliet forgot the book when she left.

I put the book away and finished this letter to you. Then I lay down on my bed. The mattress was comfortable, and the sheets smelled clean and sweet. I shut my eyes for a moment, and when I opened them, I heard Linda calling me to come downstairs for dinner. Then I closed my eyes again. I heard a gentle tap on the door.

"Dinner's ready," said Miles.

"Dinner's ready," said Flora.

"I think I'm going to sleep through it," I said. I knew I should probably eat something. Since breakfast with my dad, I'd only had that sandwich Linda made. And it had been a long day. It seemed like years had passed since my dad and I had eggs and hash browns and toast in a diner near the docks. But even though my stomach was growling, I couldn't seem to keep my eyes open. I slept through the night.

I dreamed I was on the boat again, and the seagull was still shrieking. Only this time it seemed to be screaming Lucy Lucy Lucy. . . .

I remember waking up and thinking, I don't know anyone named Lucy. The dawn was just beginning to lighten the sky. I heard seagulls, real ones. Then I fell back asleep.

I'll write again tomorrow. Meanwhile, sweet dreams.

Love,

Jack

DEAR DAD,

You'd like it here. The house is really nice, but to be honest, it could use a lot of work, and you'd be the perfect guy for the job. I'm just getting to know the kids. They're very polite and nice, and I think it's going to be fine. But they're still a little shy around me. So far. I'm sure they'll warm up when we get to know each other better. I'll write more when I get more time. I'm still sort of tired from the trip yesterday.

Love,

Jack

DEAR SOPHIE,

My first morning on the island was warm and sunny. The ocean light makes you feel like . . . it's hard to explain. Like everything is transparent, like you not only see everything clearly but you can almost see through everything. Like I said, it's hard to explain. Through my windows I heard the cries of the seagulls, and now they sounded very different than they did on the ferry, when I had that stupid hallucination about the bird calling my name. In the morning, the birds sounded cheerful, and their voices filled me with energy. Almost as if I was flying, too. Isn't it amazing how different everything looks in the morning? The house no longer seemed creepy, and when I thought about the children, I remembered how pretty they are, and I couldn't understand why I'd imagined they were little vampires keeping all sorts of horrible secrets.

The smell of coffee found its way up to my room in the attic. I got dressed and followed it down to the kitchen. The halls seemed a lot brighter than they had the afternoon before. I passed the room with the pool table and also several huge rooms I would have noticed if I'd seen them, so I figured the doors must have been closed yesterday. Maybe they had been locked, but now someone had unlocked them.

Except for that one room where the corridor had dead-ended and the kids had tried the door and then exchanged those funny glances. I passed it on the way to breakfast, and—I couldn't help rattling the doorknob—it was still locked. Probably Linda just forgot to unlock that one. Or maybe it was some kind of storeroom. But why had the kids tried to open it? I'll find out sooner or later.

Anyhow, there were certainly enough rooms for me to check out now. One of them was the library, and I stopped in the doorway and looked at all the books and at the little rolling wooden staircase for reaching the highest shelves. Something about the beauty of the library and how many books there were made me feel really eager to read, and I couldn't wait to get some free time so I could go back there and explore.

The kids were waiting for me in the kitchen. Maybe it was just the clothes they were wearing yesterday that had made them seem so odd and old-fashioned. Because today, dressed in jeans and T-shirts, they almost looked like regular kids.

Linda had made a huge platter of scrambled eggs and toast, and the kids were helping themselves and digging in. Linda heaped a plate with food and passed it to me down the table. A slight breeze in the window blew a crystal teardrop, which sprinkled rainbows all over the walls, and suddenly the whole scene seemed . . . normal. The two kids and Linda, who by now might as well have been their mom. And me, the babysitter whom their kindly uncle had hired and brought to this pretty island to hang out with them for the summer.

The kids were eager to show me around the

grounds. Linda packed some sandwiches and a thermos full of orange juice and put them in a backpack,
which Miles slid on, like any kid going off to school.
And if the kids said, "Let's go!" at the precise same
moment, it seemed more like a coincidence than
like a sign of some eerie telepathic communication.

We left through the tall front door, and when I
walked onto the wraparound porch, the sight of the
ocean and the lawns dotted with red poppies rolling
down to the shore was so gorgeous that it seemed
like the breath was being sucked out of my chest,
and for a second I felt dizzy.

"Wow!" I said. The kids looked at me, puzzled.
"It's amazing." I pointed at the sea.

"It *is* pretty, isn't it?" Flora said. "We hardly
notice anymore."

In the bright morning light, the black house had
a reddish cast that made it look less alarming. As I
followed the kids past the clay tennis courts, I told
them how you and I used to play sometimes. Flora
didn't seem to know what tennis *was*. Miles said
he remembered seeing some old wooden rackets in

the attic somewhere. Maybe we could find them and play, if I wanted. But he didn't sound all that enthusiastic.

"I could teach you!" I said.

"That would be lovely," said Flora politely, but she didn't seem excited about it.

We passed a dilapidated windmill and the large brick structure that, Miles explained, housed the propane-fueled generator that powered the island. Then we headed toward a marsh thick with tall reeds and crisscrossed by a wooden walkway that zigzagged over the bog.

"Awesome boardwalk!" I said. "What's with the zigzag, anyway?"

Miles and Flora looked at each other, and for the first time that morning, I remembered how often they'd exchanged those knowing, slightly disturbing glances the afternoon before.

Miles said, "I believe the ancient Chinese used to build them that way in order to confuse the evil spirits." I looked at him, wondering where he'd learned that.

We spent a long time running back and forth along the zigzags. I told the kids to be careful not to fall in, but Flora only giggled.

Beyond the bog was a moss garden with rocks that looked like mountains, and clumps of moss like tiny forests. Then I found myself on another lawn, like a brilliant green sky dotted with cloud forms of tiny white flowers.

"Look!" said Miles, and I glanced up to see a giant hawk above us. I watched it catching the currents over the meadow. It looked so delighted to be up there, doing its dips and whirls and glides, that it seemed like a good sign about my summer with Miles and Flora. How could I have been so ridiculously nervous? What had I been worried about?

We wound up on the shore of the lake. On the opposite bank was a wooden boathouse, decorated, like the main house, like a gingerbread castle, though in this case, more like a dollhouse. Moored to the dock was the little rowboat I'd seen from my window, and I helped the kids untie the heavy ropes that kept it from floating away.

Flora said, "Let's have our picnic out on the lake."

It hadn't been all that long since breakfast, but I said, "Sure, why not?" We could hang out and talk awhile before we ate lunch. Get to know each other.

Miles and Flora and I took turns rowing, and in no time we were in the middle of the lake. We rested our oars against the sides of the boat and leaned back and drifted. I asked the kids what they liked to do for fun, and for some reason—maybe they didn't understand the concept of fun—both of them thought I was asking what their future plans were. Flora said she wanted to be a botanist or a horticulturalist, and she told me she was learning the names of every plant on the island. She said she would tell me them sometime, if she and I went for a walk without Miles, who thought plants were boring. Miles told me he wanted to travel, and he listed, in a dreamy voice, all the countries he wanted to visit.

Outer Mongolia was at the top of the list.

"Why Outer Mongolia?" I said.

"Because—" said Flora.

"Be quiet, Flora," Miles said, and Flora fell silent. I let it go but decided that at some point I'd have to have a talk with Miles about being rude to his sister.

After that I did most of the talking. I told them all about you and my dad. They didn't ask about my mom, maybe because they could tell that I didn't want to talk about it. If we did, they might start thinking sad thoughts about their own parents. When I finally ran out of things to say, I asked Miles how he liked school.

He said, "It's good. I like it a lot. Let's eat our sandwiches now."

The sandwiches were delicious—ham and cheese and some kind of butter with fresh herbs. And homemade chocolate-chip cookies that tasted especially great with the orange juice we drank from the cap of the thermos we passed around. It felt comfortable and friendly, as if we'd known each other longer than we had. Flora neatly folded the paper in which the sandwiches had been wrapped, and Miles just as neatly put the paper and the thermos into the backpack, to take home.

After a while I felt sleepy, and the children looked like they could use a nap.

Miles said, "Let's row to that shady patch." It was still warm, but we were out of the sun, and all three of us dozed off. Maybe the sun and rocking of the boat had knocked us out, or maybe it was the strain of trying to get to know each other.

When we woke up, the sun had moved in the sky. It was late afternoon. We rowed back in and tied up the boat, and with the children skipping ahead, we made our way back to the house. We found Linda in the vegetable garden alongside the house, picking peas from a row of tall vines that grew along a mesh fence.

Linda's garden was lush and beautiful. All the plants and vegetables grew in neat rows with straw between them and mulched paths you could clearly see so you didn't step off and accidentally trample the broccoli, like I did sometimes in my dad's garden. I wished my dad could see Linda's garden. He would really like it and maybe even learn something about gardening.

But there is one peculiar thing about Linda's garden. Instead of wooden or metal posts marking the vegetable rows, she has golf clubs sticking out of the ground at the end of every furrow.

"What's with the golf clubs?" I asked.

Linda said, "They belonged to my husband, and after he died, I didn't know what to do with them. I couldn't bring myself to throw them out because he'd loved them so much, and then I got the idea of using them as row markers in the garden." I guess she thinks it's sort of funny or touching, sentimental or practical, I can't really tell. But the truth—which of course I would never say to Linda—is that they're kind of ugly, all these rusting golf clubs sticking out of the ground.

"Cool recycling idea," I said.

"Did you guys have a good day?" she said. "It looks like Miles and Flora got a little sun."

The kids nodded, and I did, too. And I was pretty sure they meant they'd enjoyed themselves, which made me feel hopeful about the two months ahead.

Linda handed me a pea pod.

"Go ahead, taste it," she said. Inside were five perfect green bombs of crunchiness and sugar.

"Fresh pea pasta for dinner?" Linda said.

"Awesome," said Miles and Flora.

Linda made homemade pasta, and chicken breasts pounded thin and fried in butter. I could tell how much the kids liked being in the kitchen when Linda cooked, sitting at the long wooden table and helping her measure flour and shell peas. I held down the pasta machine so it wouldn't shake the table as Linda cranked out the sheets of dough, which got thinner and thinner each time she fed them through. Maybe it was the promise of dinner, but the kids were almost chatty, telling Linda how much I'd liked the zigzag walkway and how tasty the sandwiches she'd packed for our lunch were and how I'd promised to teach them to play tennis if we could find the rackets in the attic.

After dinner the kids and Linda and I played Scrabble. Linda won, and I came in second, but I couldn't help noticing that the kids knew an awful lot of long, obscure words for children their age.

Finally, Linda said, "Bedtime." The kids stood up and kissed Linda on the cheek and shook my hand and said good night and left. By then I shouldn't have been surprised by their superpoliteness, but I couldn't help thinking of your little brothers and of the screaming racket they made that night when I was having dinner at your house and your mom said they had to go to bed.

After they left, Linda said, "I adore those kids."

"I can tell," I said.

"I adore them," she repeated, "but even so, this is my favorite time of the day. In the winter I sit by the fire. In summer there's the screened porch. Let's go out on the porch."

Linda and I took a pot of chamomile tea out on the porch and sat in the comfortable rocking chairs while around us moths and June bugs bashed themselves against the screens. Because we were far from the electric lights of the nearest city or town, the stars seemed especially brilliant, like tiny holes punched in the black sky so that the brightness could shine through. I could pick out all the constellations you showed me that night we went to the beach, and it made me happy to think about you, and to think that this was the same ocean you and I had waded into, holding hands, freezing our feet in the water, which was way too cold for swimming.

After a while I said, "Linda, can you tell me a little bit more about the kids? Mr. Crackstone didn't say much and I don't want to bring up anything that's going to upset them."

In a quiet voice, Linda filled in the story I'd heard from Jim Crackstone. Their parents had been traveling to visit the mom's family in Varanasi, India, when they'd been killed in the train wreck. It was really remarkable, Linda said, how well-adjusted Miles and Flora were, considering how suddenly they'd been orphaned and their uncle's decision to raise them on the island, in complete isolation, without TV or movies or other children to play with, taught by a series of tutors, some of who had been excellent while others had been . . . Linda hesitated.

"Problematic," she said at last.

I wanted to ask what the problems had been. In fact I wondered again how I could turn the conversation to the subject of the deaths and the investigation that the blind man's wife had mentioned. I knew I should let it drop, but something in this place made me uncomfortable. I've never believed in ghosts before, or anything supernatural. You know that. And yet I couldn't shake the uneasy feeling I'd had since I set foot on the ferry.

But it was so calm and peaceful on the porch in the beautiful warm night that I began to think that the blind man's wife had gotten it wrong. Probably she was thinking of some other island altogether. Anyhow, I didn't want to ruin the mood and the nice time I was having with Linda.

Linda told me how glad she was that this year Miles had gone off the island to go to school. Though Flora had missed her brother terribly, she also was very excited, because the school experience had gone so well for Miles that their uncle had started talking about eventually, though not immediately, sending Flora away, too.

"What will you do then?" I asked Linda. "If they both go away."

"I like solitude," she said. "And I'll be happy to see them come home for vacations and in the summer."

Then Linda talked about her husband and how much she missed him and how hard it had been for her to see him die slowly of a kidney ailment.

She said, "He died here on the island. I insisted on taking care of him till the end. It was fine with the children's uncle, but you wouldn't believe how difficult the authorities on the mainland made it for me."

So that was it! I wanted to say. The blind man's wife had thought that some horrific crime had happened here, when the so-called problem had been Linda's brave insistence on letting her husband die at home, surrounded by people who loved him. Not only did hearing the truth make me like and admire Linda even more but I was relieved to learn that at least one of the scary stories people told about the island was based on a terrible misunderstanding of something tragic—but innocent and loving, all the same.

Linda said, "He's buried in the family graveyard at the other end of the island. So I guess I'm here forever, whether I want to be or not."

Then I told Linda how my mom had died suddenly, in the school yard, at recess. She'd been a teacher. I sometimes wished she'd died at home with my dad and me there, so she wouldn't have been alone, though my dad told me the whole thing had happened too fast for her to know what was happening. Linda said she was sorry, and I said I was sorry about her husband.

After that there wasn't much to say, but still it felt good to sit there in the silence and watch the stars blinking their secret messages at one another. It was all so peaceful and comforting, the steady rocking of our chairs, the buzzing of the insects, and beyond that the quiet, calming splash of the waves against the beach.

Just describing it is making me feel calm and

relaxed. So I guess I'll shut this down for now and go to bed and write you again tomorrow.

Have a good sleep.

Love,

Jack

DEAR SOPHIE,

A week has gone by since I got here, and it's been amazingly pleasant. Mostly I play with the children. Sure enough, we found the old tennis rackets Miles thought he'd seen, and they work all right—well, they kind of work—with the dead tennis balls we found lying around near the rackets. There's not a lot of bounce to the tennis balls, so everything goes pretty slowly, which is just as well.

Miles is not exactly the world's most athletic kid. Flora's pretty coordinated, but you can tell she hasn't spent a lot of time playing strenuous games. She gets tired easily, or maybe she just gets bored and says she's tired. We searched for the pool cues for a while, but we couldn't find any, which was probably just as well, because when I offered to teach the kids to play pool, they gave each other those funny looks again and said they really didn't want to.

I've learned my way around the house, which no longer seems like the confusing maze it did when I first got here. Everything's wide open now . . . except for that one room that's still kept locked. Every so often I pass by it and turn the knob just to see. I kind of wonder what's in there. But I've never found the right moment to ask Linda, and I don't want to seem nosy and pushy. If Linda has the room sealed off, there's probably a good reason. I have to say it's a good thing that Linda's so nice and normal. If I was stuck out here with a nasty cook and two odd kids and a locked room, I'd probably think it was one of those secret chambers like in this horror movie I saw where the evil king killed one wife after another and kept their bodies in the cellar, where he would go and hang out and have formal dinners with their corpses as if they were all still alive.

But it's not like that here. In fact it's more like a cheery sitcom called *Crackstone's Landing* than like a slasher film. I hang out with the kids, eat good food, spend the evenings chatting with Linda. I write you letters whenever I can. I send my letters off on the ferry, and I keep waiting to get one back from you. I try not to wonder why you haven't written me back so far. I'm sure you're busy. Or something. I refuse to let it upset me.

Anyway, I was just settling into this pleasant routine when . . . okay, I'm going to take a break and finish tomorrow so I can figure out how to tell you this part of the story without sounding crazy.

DEAR SOPHIE, PART TWO,

Okay. Here goes.

A couple of evenings after I got here, Linda and I were sitting out on the porch.

Linda said, "Did you hear that?"

"Hear what?" I asked. Then I heard it, a howl like some wild animal caught in a hideous, pain-inflicting trap. Linda was already out of her chair, tipping over the teapot as she ran into the house.

"It's Flora," she yelled.

I followed Linda to Flora's room. The lights were on, and Flora was sitting up in her pink four-poster bed, among her pink blankets and pink sheets, surrounded by pink walls and pink curtains. She was holding the side of her face, and tears were streaming down her cheeks.

"My tooth hurts," she told Linda.

It turned out that Flora had been so eager to spend the day playing with me and her brother that she hadn't told anyone that her tooth had started to bother her. And now her whole cheek was swollen, and she couldn't stop crying and begging us to please make the pain go away.

Linda got some children's aspirin and a clove to rub on Flora's gum. Before long, still weeping quietly, the poor girl dropped off to sleep. Linda said she would stay with her, in case she woke up again, and I said good night and went to my room.

The next morning Linda woke me early to explain that the ferry—which she could get to stop at the island by raising a blue flag at the end of the pier—would be there in half an hour. She was taking Flora to see the dentist on the next island over, and Miles wanted to go along. The dentist was an old friend of the children's uncle; they often played golf together. She knew that he would be willing to see Flora when they got there, even without an appointment. Then they could catch the last ferry back and be home in time for dinner. I asked if she wanted me to go along, and she said no, in fact she'd like me to stay on the island and keep an eye on the place.

The gardener, Hank Swopes, would be arriving with his crew, and though Linda would leave a note explaining what needed to be done, she would feel more comfortable if I was there to greet Hank and his men when they arrived. It didn't make sense to me. I was sure the gardener knew way more about the island than I did, and to tell the truth, I was a little uneasy about being left alone. What if something went wrong? I told myself that nothing was going to go wrong. Besides which, I wouldn't be alone. The gardener would be here, and by the time he left, Linda and the kids would be back.

"I'll be fine!" I told Linda.

"Why wouldn't you be?" she said.

Linda's shiny red truck headed down the road to the pier, and I kept waving long after they could no longer see me. I went back into the huge black house, which suddenly seemed extremely noisy in the silence. The floors creaked beneath my feet as I walked over the carpets, and the ticking of the clocks sounded much louder than I remembered, and somehow ominous.

I wandered around, and after a while I found myself in a long corridor where I'd never been before. The walls were lined with portraits—of the children's ancestors, I guessed—and the eyes of the stern-looking men and women seemed to watch me disapprovingly as I passed. I told myself it was just an optical illusion and that I should enjoy this opportunity to be alone, to *really* figure out my way around and to look at things that I might have felt self-conscious examining closely if Linda and the kids were there.

For example, the family photos, framed and arranged on the bookshelves and the end tables in one of the sitting rooms. One picture showed a group of people in turbans and saris, with a very beautiful woman standing in the front row beside a tall man who looked a little like Jim Crackstone. I realized that it was probably a wedding picture of the children's parents with their mom's family in India.

A couple of other photos showed Jim Crackstone with Miles and Flora, two little toddlers who looked so dazed and tragic that I assumed the pictures were taken soon after their parents were killed. Linda was in some of the shots, also with the kids. In some of them Linda was arm in arm with a handsome guy who I guessed was her husband. Then there was one photo of Linda's husband looking much thinner and older, and after that he disappeared from the pictures.

There were a few fairly recent photos of Miles and Flora, one of which drew my attention, not because of what it showed—the kids standing on the shore of the lake, in front of the boathouse, with stiff, posed smiles on their faces—but because, unlike the others, it was mounted crookedly and creased and sort of bunched up as if it had been taken out of its frame and hastily stuffed back in.

When I picked it up, the glass fell out of the frame, and the creased photo also slipped out.

There was another picture concealed beneath the first. In the hidden photo, the children (looking around the same age as they are now, maybe a year or so younger) were standing on the lakeshore, near the boathouse. Only in this one they were standing beside two adults, a man and a woman. The woman was wearing a long dress, the man a formal, old-fashioned black suit, but that was all I could see of them. Because their faces had been scratched out, as if someone had taken a knife or the point of a scissors and slashed away at the paper until nothing remained but jagged holes where their faces should have been.

Well! That gave me a creepy feeling! Who were the mystery man and woman? What had they done, and why did someone hate them enough to obliterate their faces? It didn't seem like something Linda would do, but I didn't know her that well. Could it have been Miles or Flora, with their perfect manners and their gentle little voices? I figured I could ask Linda about it when I got to know her better, but something told me I'd have to wait and find the right moment. It was also possible that Linda didn't even know about the mutilated photo, and I didn't want to upset her. It sure upset me.

It seemed wiser, at least for a while, to pretend—even to myself!—that I hadn't seen it. I carefully replaced it under the other photo and put both pictures back in the frame. Then I decided it might be a good idea to make myself some breakfast.

The sunny kitchen cheered me up. I scrambled some eggs and made some toast, and as I sat at the table, eating the food, which turned out to be delicious, I noticed that I was enjoying the solitude. It no longer felt like a nervous loneliness but like space and . . . freedom! Once more, I felt hopeful about the summer ahead. The image of the ruined photo crept back into my mind, but . . . so what? Kids did weird things all the time. They could be destructive without meaning to, without knowing what they were doing. And just because Miles and Flora said please and thank you didn't mean they weren't kids.

Just as I was washing up my breakfast dishes, I heard the put-put-put of a boat, and a few minutes later I looked out the window and saw a bunch of guys in work clothes, laughing and joking as they walked across the lawn toward the house.

Mr. Swopes, who told me to call him Hank, wore jeans and a beard and had a warm, friendly handshake. Actually, he reminded me a little of my dad. He looked surprised to see me instead of Linda, but without too much confusion I explained the situation. He seemed disappointed that Linda wasn't there, in a way that made me think that maybe he had a crush on Linda. I handed him the "to do" list that Linda had left on the kitchen table. Hank laughed when he read it and said, "I can see that me and the guys have our work cut out for us today. I guess we'll see you around." I asked if they wanted some water or something to eat. But Hank said no, thanks, they'd brought their lunch and plenty of water with them.

The men began trimming the shrubs and mowing the lawn near the house, and I watched them, feeling a little envious of how smoothly they worked together and what good friends they obviously were. Each one of them seemed to know what the others were doing, or were about to do, without having to talk. When their chores took them farther out toward the lake, I decided to go to the library and see if I could find something interesting to read.

The library was on the main floor, with tall glass doors through which you could walk onto the patio at the back of the house. The light shining through the tall windows was dusty and soft, and the smell of old paper and leather and books was soothing. Glinting gold letters caught my eye, and I took down the plays of William Shakespeare and spent a while, sitting on the floor, looking at an engraving of Hamlet holding a skull. Then I skimmed through another book about the Roman Empire, and as I put it away, I noticed that beside it was a book about volcanoes. I recalled the prints of volcanoes on Jim Crackstone's office wall. For a moment it seemed like another coincidence, until I realized that Jim Crackstone had grown up in this house. Maybe his love for volcanoes had started when he was a boy.

I began reading about what volcanoes are and why they become active and about the most famous volcano eruptions in history. It was so engrossing that hours must have gone by without my being aware of how much time was passing. I'd just begun reading a chapter on how Pompeii was completely buried by the lava from Mount Vesuvius when I heard a voice in the hall. I jumped.

Hank called, "I guess we'll be getting on our way now. Tell Linda we'll see her next week."

"Bye. Thanks! See you," I told Hank. I walked to the window to watch the gardeners go, all of them laughing and kidding around. I listened to the sound of Hank's motorboat starting up, then fading away over the water. For a moment I felt lonely and nervous . . . and then the anxiousness passed.

I looked at my watch. It was almost five. Linda and the kids would be home soon. I hoped Flora was feeling better.

I returned to my volcano book, and soon I was reading about how the citizens of Pompeii were wiped out. I looked at pictures of the ruined buildings, and then at gruesome photos of the casts of bodies created by lava that had hardened around whole families, who had died in agony, trying to escape. Suddenly, I had this feeling. . . . I don't know how to describe it except to say that I sensed the presence of a presence. The only thing I can compare it to is one night when a bat flew into my dad's house. The hairs on my arms and the back of my neck stood straight up, and I *knew* that the bat was there long before I saw it swooping around our living room, and I yelled, and Dad got a broom and chased it out the front door.

Crazy goose bumps rose on my skin as I turned and looked toward the windows.

A man was standing on the other side of the glass

doors, looking in. I could tell that he was looking for someone. Someone in particular, and he wasn't looking for me. I can't explain why I was so sure, especially because the light was behind him, so that at first all I saw was his silhouette.

I figured that Hank or one of his men had come back to get something they'd left behind. But the man at the window wasn't Hank or one of the other gardeners. The angle of the sun shifted, and I was able to see him more clearly.

The strange thing was that I was sure I'd seen him before. He had longish hair and was tall and barrel-chested, wearing a black old-fashioned suit, which made me think of the guy with the scratched-out face in the hidden photo. But that wasn't where I recognized him from, and anyway, the man in the photo had no face. I'd seen him somewhere else . . . but where?

The sweetest sound I ever heard was the rattle of Linda's truck coming up the driveway.

When I looked back, the man outside the window had vanished.

I know it's not the manliest thing to admit, but my legs were shaking as I got up from the floor. But even with my knees knocking, I felt weirdly brave. I was the man of the house now.

I ran to the French doors and threw them open. There was no one around, no one walking across the lawns that went on for so long that the guy would have had to be airlifted out of there to disappear so fast. He wasn't anywhere. Of course he wasn't. There was no one else on the island. The gardeners had gone home. And I'd imagined I'd seen someone. Or maybe it was a trick of the sun, the shadow of a tree. Or, okay, I'll say it—maybe the house is haunted.

I'm joking about the haunted part. I hope you know that, Sophie.

I left the library, slamming the door. Even if I was seeing things, I had the strange idea that if I kept the library shut off from the rest of the house, I could keep the hallucination, or whatever it was, contained in that one room. Obviously, I realize that ghosts can walk through walls. But I took a deep breath and reminded myself: I don't believe in ghosts.

I can't tell you how much I wish I'd get a letter from you.

Love,

Jack

DEAR JACK,

I'm glad you're having a fairly nice time and don't feel too isolated on the island. As you know, I was really angry at my dad for asking his friend Jim Crackstone to get you that job and pay you all that money just so my father would have a clever way to keep us apart for the summer.

I never liked Jim Crackstone. But you already know that. Anyhow, the kids you're taking care of sound interesting, and you'll probably be really good for them. They'll be less lonely with you there. Just like I would be less lonely if you were here. Which you're not. I keep telling myself that the weeks will go by quickly, and you'll come back with all that money, so we can go to the same college. That's what we need to remember whenever we miss each other. Which is all the time, right?

That story about the seagull screaming at you on the ferry was so scary! I couldn't sleep the night after I read it. And that blind couple on the boat, and that woman crying on deck . . . I wonder if the island is really haunted, like people say. Well, I guess you'll find out. And that's got to be more interesting compared to what I'm doing here, working in the boring town public library, where they don't even really need me, but they're doing my dad a favor because he gives the library money. At least I get to hang out with our friends after work and on weekends, though all the things you and I used to do—the beach parties and picnics and stuff—will just seem dull without you.

I wish I had more to tell you, but unlike you, I'm having a totally uneventful summer. Write to me soon. Have a good time but not such a good time that you forget me.

Love,

Sophie

DEAR SOPHIE,

I was so happy to hear from you! Please write me again, right away, and tell me more about every little thing you're doing. Maybe it seems boring to you, but I'm sure your summer must be exciting compared to what I'm doing here. Unless you count seeing ghosts.

I decided not to mention my little . . . hallucination to Linda and the kids. Linda still doesn't know me that well, and it won't make her all that comfortable to think that the children's new companion is a guy who imagines strange men peering in the library window.

When Linda got back from taking Flora to the dentist, the children went to their rooms. Linda said they were tired from the trip and wanted to take a nap before dinner. She asked me if everything had been okay in her absence, and I said I'd enjoyed having all that time and privacy to roam around and explore. I told her I'd spent a lot of the day reading in the library.

When I mentioned that Hank seemed disappointed that she wasn't there and that he'd said to be sure to tell her he'd see her next week, Linda smiled to herself. Maybe I was right about there being something between them.

Linda told me she'd gone by the post office and picked up the mail, which otherwise wouldn't have come on the ferry till later in the week. She smiled again as she said that one of the letters was for me, and she kept smiling as I ripped the envelope open and stood right there in the kitchen reading your letter over and over.

After a while, Linda said, "Don't you want to know how Flora is?"

"Oh, I'm sorry," I said. "I got distracted. What happened at the dentist?"

"Don't worry," said Linda. "I still remember what young love is like."

It's always a little embarrassing when grown-ups talk that way, but somehow it was less creepy coming from Linda. I thought of the poetry book I'd found in my room, and I wondered if it had been a present from Linda's husband.

"Anyhow," Linda was saying, "Flora's fine. She's still a little spacey from the anesthetic. Dr. Jacobs had to pull an impacted baby tooth."

"Poor Flora!" I said.

"She was a brave little soldier," said Linda. "I'm making soft foods for dinner. Mashed potatoes for Flora and some kind of veal stew for Miles and you and me. Flora can have gravy on her potatoes if she wants."

"Are you okay?" I asked Linda.

"Fine," she said. "Why wouldn't I be?"

"I don't know why I asked," I said. Linda wasn't her normal cheerful self. She looked worried or just distracted. Well, it must have been stressful, taking a little girl with a raging toothache to get dental surgery and get back to the island.

I kept Linda company while she cooked dinner. The children came downstairs and immediately started chattering about their trip to the neighboring island. If Flora was still woozy from whatever the dentist gave her, I couldn't tell.

The kids described all the passengers on the ferry and an enormous Great Dane they'd seen waiting outside the post office for its owner, and the funny eyeglasses that Dr. Jacobs's receptionist wore. I acted as if I agreed that they were amazing things to see, though, to tell the truth, what impressed the kids wasn't all that exciting. But I knew it was a treat for them to see *anything* they didn't see every day on the island. Flora did an imitation of how the dentist's voice sounded when she was coming out from under the anesthesia. Linda asked if her tooth hurt now.

Flora said, "Not very much."

All through dinner, I had the feeling that Linda was worried about something. I still didn't know her that well, so maybe it was nothing. Just something else I imagined. But from time to time I'd catch a look in her eyes that reminded me of the way my dad looks when a job isn't going well or a client is giving him a hard time about paying a bill.

After the kids went off to bed, Linda asked if I wanted to go out on the porch. I'd been looking forward to drinking more chamomile tea and maybe finishing the conversation—though I couldn't remember where we'd left off—that Linda and I had been having when we'd been interrupted by Flora's howl of pain.

We rocked in silence for a while, sipping our tea. Then Linda said, "I know you practically just got here, and I don't want to burden you with this. I probably shouldn't mention it at all, but I need to tell someone."

So I'd been right. Linda did have something on her mind. The first thing that occurred to me was that maybe the dentist had said that Flora needed lots of dental work or braces. Her teeth looked straight enough to me, but I'm no expert.

Linda said, "I need to figure out how to deal with this. As I'm sure you know, Jim Crackstone has made it very clear that he doesn't want to be bothered with good or bad news about the kids. Not ever. Not about anything."

"I did kind of get that impression," I said. But Linda didn't laugh.

She said, "There was another letter in the mail. I don't know why it came here instead of directly to their uncle. Maybe because Jim Crackstone has informed everyone involved that the less he hears about the kids, the better he likes it. The letter was from Miles's school. It said they were sorry, but they don't want Miles returning to school in the fall."

"Why not?" I said. "Were his grades bad? I'll bet it was hard for him to adjust to being away from the island and you and his sister. After my mom died I practically failed out of elementary school. He was probably homesick, and his schoolwork suffered. I know Jim Crackstone doesn't want to be bothered, but I'm sure if he talks to someone at the school they'll give Miles another chance—"

"His grades were excellent," interrupted Linda.

"Then what?"

Linda's voice was so soft, I had to lean close to hear. "They said that he was a bad influence on the other boys."

"What kind of bad influence? How could that be possible? Miles is the most polite kid I've ever met.

I've never heard him curse, not once—"

Linda said, "They used the word *evil*. They said he'd had an evil influence over the others."

"*Evil?*" I said. "*Miles?* It's a mix-up. They've got the wrong kid. He's not evil; they're crazy! What could he have done?"

"That's what I think about Miles," said Linda. "And that's what I can't figure out."

"Can't you ask Miles?" I said. "I'm sure it must be a mistake."

"I don't want to," said Linda. "Not yet. I still can't believe it. And I don't want to upset him."

In the silence, broken only by the rocking of our chairs and the buzzing of the June bugs against the screens, I wondered if it was true. But e*vil* is a strong word. I knew that Linda was wondering, too.

Suddenly, I remembered the ruined photo in the library. And the blind man talking about the island being haunted—and about the investigation. And, okay, the seagull's warning. Plus I couldn't help thinking about the man I'd imagined at the window. I tried to put it out of my mind.

I said, "Linda, who was here before me? Who taught the kids before I got here?"

"I thought their uncle told you. A very nice girl named Kate. But she left to get married and didn't warn us and left us in the lurch."

"And before Kate?" I said. "Who was here before Kate?"

"Before Kate?" Linda rocked back in her chair and took a swallow of tea. "That's a longer story. I hope you're not tired."

"I'm not tired at all," I said.

"Then I'll tell you," Linda said. "His name was Norris Holmes. The children's uncle hired him when my husband became too ill to do the hard work on the island. Norris was a general handyman and gardener.

"I never liked him, though, at least at the start. I couldn't figure out why. I always had the feeling that there was something about his life that he didn't want anyone knowing. But he was a good worker and very helpful with keeping up the place while I took care of the children and, more and more, of my husband. One thing I never trusted about him was that he was always talking about the exotic places he'd been—he'd climbed Mount Kilimanjaro; he'd trekked through Outer Mongolia. But sometimes I would ask him a question that he couldn't answer, and I'd get the feeling that he was making it all up.

"For several years, the children had a part-time teacher, a Miss Eldridge, who left to teach third grade in an elementary school on the mainland. Working in his usual mysterious ways, Jim Crackstone hired a full-time governess, a woman named Lucy."

For a moment I spaced out. The seagull in my dream had said, Lucy Lucy Lucy. I don't usually remember my dreams, but this one had stuck with me. . . .

Linda said, "I knew there would be trouble from the very first time I'd introduced Norris to Lucy. Lucy was pretty, pale, with bright red hair—"

"Redheaded?" I remembered the woman on the boat, and a chill went down my spine. I told myself that lots of people had red hair. Miles, for example.

"Miles was thrilled," said Linda. "To tell the truth, I'm not sure he'd ever met another redhead before."

"What did Norris look like?" I said. I can't explain why, but I was already praying, Please don't let him look like the guy I saw at the library window.

"Dark-haired. Tall."

I thought: Like the guy at the window. But lots of guys were tall and dark-haired.

Linda said, "I guess some women would have thought Norris was handsome. The problem was, Norris thought he was handsome, and men who can't get over themselves just aren't my type.

"Later, looking back, I remembered thinking that Norris and Lucy recognized something in each other, the first minute they met. I had no idea what it was, but I didn't like it. Or maybe that was something I began to think only after what happened later.

"Otherwise, Lucy was pleasant and intelligent, and it's possible that she would have worked out fine if it hadn't been for Norris. She'd been to college, and she took the children's lessons seriously. Until then, their education had been kind of spotty, though both kids were natural readers. In that way, at least, maybe their uncle was right about the benefits of their having nothing else to do on the island. Without video games or the internet or TV, the children had no choice but to learn to read—and like it.

"Lucy made sure the children knew the basics of arithmetic, and she taught them geography and a little bit of science. She had a real passion for plants and botany, and she used to advise Norris about what would grow best in the gardens."

Linda paused and rocked awhile, sipping her tea, obviously trying to decide how to tell me the next part of the story.

I said, "Miles wants to travel to Mongolia. And Flora wants to be a botanist when she grows up."

Linda gave me a quick look. "Well, that would have been the best part of Lucy and Norris's influence."

"And the worst part?" I asked.

Linda fell silent for a long time. I listened to the furious buzzing of a June bug that was just not getting the message that he couldn't fly through the screen and join us on the porch.

"I never exactly knew," Linda said. "I guess it was partly my fault, leaving the kids alone with them. But at that point, I'll be honest with you, Jack. I had a lot on my plate. Let's just say I wasn't giving the situation here my complete attention. There were so many trips to the mainland, to see doctors and spend time in hospitals before my husband died. I guess I could have taken the kids with me, but it would have been awful for them. They were close to my husband; they liked him. And why would I take them, when Jim Crackstone was paying two other people to look after the children? The truth is, I was grateful to have someone to leave them with.

"By then it was pretty clear that Norris and Lucy had fallen in love. Or fallen in *something*. Looking back, I wouldn't dignify whatever was going on between them by calling it love, exactly. But I could sense something sparking back and forth every time I saw them together. At first it was just the way that Lucy looked at Norris when he told his crazy stories about getting captured by bandits in the Atlas Mountains of Morocco and having to tread water in the Black Sea when his boat hit a rock and sank. Often, after the children were in bed, I'd see Lucy hurrying across the lawns in the direction of the gardener's cottage, where Norris lived." Linda paused.

"Have the kids ever taken you there?" she asked me. "To the cottage?"

"No," I said. "They never mentioned there was a cottage."

"I'm not surprised," Linda said.

"Where is it?" I said.

"On the other side of the lake and the tennis courts," Linda said. "Hidden back in the woods."

I remembered how the very first day, when the children had taken me around the island, they'd made a wide circle around the tennis court. Had they been keeping me from the cottage? What would have happened if I'd asked to go that way?

"Right from the start," Linda said, "Norris and Lucy kept their relationship secret. Maybe they thought that the children's uncle had some policy prohibiting on-the-job romance. Though they should have known that the children's uncle didn't have much of a policy about anything, really, except about not giving him any trouble.

"Maybe it sounds a little paranoid, but I sensed something dark, like a storm cloud hovering over Norris and Lucy, something that gave me a very different feeling from the warm sensation you get when you see two nice people falling in love. One problem was that Norris was so much older than Lucy. He had all the power. Sometimes, in the mornings, I noticed that Lucy's eyes were red, as if she'd been crying all night.

"But one thing about Lucy and Norris that I found reassuring—maybe too reassuring, as it turned out—was that they were always discreet around the kids. As far as I knew, the children never suspected that Norris and Lucy were involved. Or maybe it's just how kids are: Miles and Flora seemed to assume that the only reason Norris and Lucy even talked to each other was because of them.

"Or anyway, that was how it seemed."

Something about the way Linda sighed—I could tell she was asking herself how she could have missed the first signs of trouble.

"At first Miles and Flora liked being left with Norris and Lucy when my husband and I had to leave the island. But eventually I started noticing that the children were acting oddly. They had nightmares; they refused to eat. For the first time ever, Miles punched his sister hard, on the arm, and Flora wept, on and off, for a whole day. They always acted especially strange when I first got home from the mainland.

"They seemed nervous, sort of . . . shifty. I began to see Miles giving Flora that silencing look when Flora was about to say something, and what worried me was that I was sure I'd seen Norris give Lucy the same look. The kids had always been totally open with me before, but now I had the feeling that they were keeping secrets on top of secrets."

"I've seen them give each other that look," I said. This was the first time that Linda and I had ever suggested that Miles and Flora were anything but the most totally perfect little children. I mean, she'd used the word *unusual* . . . but somehow this was different.

"I'm sure you have." Linda sighed. "I thought they would get over it and go back to being their old sweet selves after Norris and Lucy left, but so far . . ." Her voice trailed off.

"Did you ever find out what was happening? With the kids and . . . Norris and Lucy?" For some reason, it felt strange saying their names. Maybe because I didn't know them, but I was beginning to feel as if I did.

"I told you," said Linda. "I never knew. But they had some hold over them, those two. You know me, Jack. I'm not the type to just let things go. If I think something, I say it. Especially if I'm worried, and especially if it concerns the kids.

"So I talked to them. First Norris, then Lucy. I asked if they were doing anything . . . weird or disturbing with, or in front of, the kids. They both denied it. They were insulted I'd even asked. And because I didn't have any real evidence—I'd never caught them or seen them doing anything sketchy, and the kids never said anything—I didn't know what else to do. I couldn't involve the children's uncle. . . . I decided to keep my eyes open and hope for the best.

"But the things I started noticing didn't make me feel any better. For example, they always had the kids divided up between them. Lucy was always with Flora, and Norris was always with Miles . . ."

I'd been trying not to ask, but I couldn't hold out any longer. "Linda . . . do you think they were . . . I don't know. I don't know how to say this. Molesting them or something?"

I could feel my face glowing hot. I was glad that it was night and that the only light was from the flickering citronella candles.

Linda considered her answer. "I don't think so. I hope not. The children never said anything. I read all these books and articles about how you can tell when something like that is going on. I don't know . . . my instincts told me that it wasn't. And you know what, Jack?"

"What?" I said, though I almost didn't want to hear what came next.

"This is going to sound really strange. And to tell you the truth, I'm not exactly sure what I mean when I say it. But I always had this feeling that Norris and Lucy weren't interested in the children's bodies, but rather in their souls."

"What do you mean?" I said. I felt a chill go down my back. I sort of did know what she meant.

"I told you I'm not sure," Linda said. "I can't explain. It's just something I felt. I felt something evil. . . . I know I can't say why, but that's what I felt. I tried to forget it. And I did, or almost did. But it all came back to me when Miles's school sent that letter and used the word *evil*."

"Holy shit," I said. "Sorry, Linda." Normally, I was careful not to curse around her.

"Holy shit indeed," said Linda. "Anyway, I was delighted when something happened that made it necessary to let Norris go . . ."

I said, "For harming the children?"

Linda said, "It wasn't as terrible as that, thank God. He just stole. Listen to me: he *just stole*! A silver candelabra went missing. It had been in the Crackstone family for generations. Of course Norris denied taking it, but I knew no one else could have done it. He was alone in the house on the day it disappeared. From the library."

"From the library?" I heard this loud voice inside my head saying, Hey, guess what, Linda? The strangest thing happened to me in the library the other day. I thought I saw this tall, dark-haired guy staring in the window. . . . But before I could think how to say this without seeming completely insane, Linda resumed her story.

"The nerve of that man, to think he could just take something so obvious that I was bound to notice. Something so outrageous I couldn't ignore it. Maybe he was testing me, testing my authority. I started to think he was tired of the island and wanted to blow his life here apart. I knew I should probably break Jim Crackstone's don't-bother-me rule and let him know what Norris had done, but I decided to handle it myself."

While Linda was telling me this part, my mind drifted away to the locked room. Maybe after Norris stole the silver, Linda decided to keep all the valuable stuff under lock and key. I almost wanted to tell her that she didn't have to, that with just her and me and the kids here no one would ever steal from them again. But I thought it might sound suspicious if I said, Hey, why don't you unlock your treasure room and be all trusting and open?

"Hey, Jack," Linda said, "are you listening?"

"Are you kidding?" I said. "Of course I'm listening. This is amazing."

"Wait," Linda said. "It gets more amazing. I confronted Norris about the theft one night after the kids had gone to sleep. There was a horrifying scene. Norris was yelling, threatening me. Lucy was weeping and begging me not to tell Jim. Finally Norris told me he didn't need this crappy, boring island full of dead people. He'd been wanting to get back to the bright lights and the big city where someone might be still be alive.

"I looked at Lucy to see how she was taking the fact that Norris was lumping her among the dead people. Tears were sheeting down her poor little face. I'd started not liking her and not trusting her, because I was worried about the kids. But now I just felt sorry for her for being Norris's puppet. Not that I automatically feel sorry for people who let themselves be turned into puppets. But she'd really lost her way, and she thought Norris had helped her find it. But she couldn't have been more wrong.

"The next afternoon, Norris asked me to take him to the ferry. He had a very large suitcase. I couldn't bring myself to ask if I could search it for the candelabra. But I wanted to. I was glad to see him go. Also by then my husband had died, so I could go back to taking care of the kids full-time, without the so-called help of a man I suspected of endangering their welfare.

"Norris's departure was another ugly scene. Lucy was pleading with him not to go. Right in front of the kids. I had no choice but to leave them at the house with her when I took him to the boat."

"And the kids? Were they sad when he left?"

"Well, it was strange. At first they showed no reaction to his being gone, which was pretty peculiar in itself, considering they'd spent so much time with him when he was around. Nor did they seem to mind very much when ten days, maybe two weeks, later, Lucy said she was quitting, too. She was going to the mainland to be with Norris. She announced this in a proud voice, as if she was showing me: Norris hadn't left her. He still loved her. He wanted to be with her. When she left I told her, 'Good luck. I really mean it.' And I really did.

"Every so often I asked the kids if they missed Norris and Lucy, and they always said yes, but it didn't sound like they meant it. It was like they thought it would be impolite to say no. I had to get in touch with Jim Crackstone to tell him that Lucy and Norris had gone. He was very annoyed, but he calmed down when I assured him that I could take over for a while. There was no rush for him to hire anyone else. Then he found Kate, who was perfectly competent and good with the kids, until one day she got a letter from an old boyfriend who still wanted to marry her. Six months on the island with us probably convinced her to marry the first person who asked. And now we have you. We're caught up to the present."

We rocked in silence for a long time. Then I said, "Have you heard from them since then? Did Lucy and Norris ever try to get in touch with the kids?"

"Not likely." Linda's laugh was harsh and sad—not her normal laugh. "That would be quite a trick."

"Why?" I asked.

"Because they're dead."

"No way! What happened?" I thought of the blind man and his wife, and their story about the lovers who'd been drowned when they'd tried to escape the island. Maybe the old couple had been confused. Or maybe *I'd* been confused. No, there was no maybe about it. I was really confused. Why hadn't Linda said something till now? I understood that, too. It was a time in her life that she wanted to forget. I should have made the blind man and his wife think harder until they remembered. But maybe I hadn't wanted to know.

Now I wanted to know. I needed to know.

"What happened to them?" I repeated.

"They were shot," Linda said. "In a fight in a bar on the mainland. Norris got a job bartending, which, if you ask me, was like hiring a mouse to work in a cheese factory. A mouse that got nasty when it ate cheese. And Lucy was substitute teaching in the local elementary school. Later, a woman I know at the post office said that around the time Lucy got killed the school board was getting ready to fire her anyway, because she was spending all her free time in the bar with Norris, which didn't look all that great for a teacher. . . . I can't believe you didn't read about this. It was the biggest scandal that happened on the mainland in ages."

I said, "My dad doesn't read the local paper much, and I don't watch the news all the time. . . ." I realized it was huge for Linda, and I didn't want to say that two people getting killed in a local bar fight wasn't exactly front-page news a hundred miles away.

"Norris ran a poker game in the back of the bar. Illegal. They played for high stakes. All guys. All rich. They came from a long way around. Norris always insisted on having Lucy there. The only girl. For luck, he said. Then one night some guy accused Norris of cheating. He said Lucy was helping Norris cheat. It turned into a real cowboy scene. A fight broke out; the guy pulled a gun and shot Norris and then Lucy. Two murders, and the killer only got fifteen years. Can you believe it? I don't think Norris and Lucy were any more popular in town than they were with me on the island. I think a lot of people were glad to be rid of them. Terrible story, right?"

"Wow" was all I could say.

Linda and I went back to rocking. I wanted, and I didn't want, to know what she was thinking. I said, "Remember I told you how, on the ferry, I'd heard about this couple who drowned off the island. But that was years and years ago—that was a different couple, right?"

"Another couple," Linda said. "That was decades before this. I didn't know them. I only heard. Tragic lovers must be an island tradition." She blew a stream of air between her lips.

Finally, she said, "I told you it was a long story. Mostly I try not to dwell on that period in our lives, it was so dark and sad. But like I said: when I got that letter from Miles's school, it was the first thing that crossed my mind. I blamed Norris and Lucy. Maybe after Norris and Lucy left, I should have suggested the kids get some professional counseling, in case something really did happen. But I never knew what had happened. The kids never said anything except that they liked Norris and Lucy, and they never said anything at all unless I asked."

"But you're not sure they did do anything to the kids," I said. "The kids seem normal enough. Even if they're not exactly the most ordinary kids. They've got character, right? Those looks Miles gives Flora sometimes . . . any brother and sister . . ." Did I really believe this? It was what Linda wanted to hear. And maybe it was what I wanted to believe.

"Thanks," said Linda. "I'm glad you're here, Jack. I'm going to write the school first thing tomorrow and ask them to be more specific about what they're actually accusing Miles of and what kind of proof they have. We need to get to the bottom of this."

"That sounds like a plan," I said. "Good night. See you in the morning, Linda."

"Pleasant dreams," Linda said.

And pleasant dreams to you, too, Sophie.

Love,

Jack

DEAR SOPHIE,

Isn't it bizarre how you can find out one tiny bit of information—well, maybe what Linda told me wasn't exactly tiny—but anyway, you can find out one new thing and after that the whole world looks different? It's as if you've had something wrong with your eyes, and you get new glasses, and the fuzzy outlines get sharp. Maybe sharper than you'd wanted them to be. Maybe sharper than you can stand.

By the time Linda told me about Lucy and Norris, and about Miles getting kicked out of school, I'd basically convinced myself that Miles and Flora were normal kids. A little old-fashioned, a little peculiar, but okay, what do you expect? They'd grown up practically alone on an island.

But now I've gone back to seeing them more like I did when I first met them, and all the little things about them I'd kind of stopped noticing—those funny looks they exchange, the way that Flora will start to say something, and one eyebrow twitch from Miles is all it takes to shut her up—now I notice them all the time. I'd told Linda it was just brother-sister stuff, but maybe it's more than that.

Now I've stopped trying to make excuses for them and gone completely in the other direction, and the kids seem really peculiar and maybe damaged. Secretive and strange.

Sometimes I have debates with myself. I wonder: Did Norris and Lucy do something evil to the kids? Or did nothing happen? I don't know why, but I feel like all my own weird experiences—the seagull, the scratched-out photo, to say nothing of the ghost at the library window—are starting to seem like evidence that something terrible occurred. I'm sorry, but since I set foot on the boat to come to this island, I've been feeling . . . not like myself at all. Why? What is it about this place, these kids?

More and more, I feel like I'm being paid to take care of kids who act friendly and open but who are keeping their little stash of precious secrets to themselves. If the kids were victims, I feel sorry for them. But I don't think they are. In fact they almost seem like they have this bizarre kind of power. I think they enjoy their secrets, that it makes them feel special somehow.

Only half my mind is on whatever we're supposedly doing—tennis lessons, rowing, picnics. And half my brain is trying to think of some way to ask about Norris and Lucy. I think I've become a little obsessed with Norris and Lucy.

Beyond the question of whether or not they hurt the children, it's almost as if I'm jealous. I keep thinking about how when you and I first got together, I couldn't get over the fact that you used to go out with Josh, though you always said it meant nothing. Now it's almost as if I'm jealous of Norris and Lucy for having a much bigger effect on the kids than I'll ever have. They've left the kids with a strong memory, a feeling: devotion or fear, I can't tell. But whatever it is, it's intense. No matter how many leading questions I ask, no matter what subtle way I try to pry some information loose, the kids go blank when I mention Norris and Lucy, and they give me these outer-space-alien stares. They shut me out, and I'm starting to really hate it.

Now when Flora and I take our botany walk, and she points out a flower and tells me its name, I ask, very innocently, "Oh, where did you learn that?" Flora looks at me. She knows I know something. Her eyes glaze over. It's almost as if she's hearing Miles, even though he isn't there. And then she'll say something like "I don't remember" or "I read it in a book."

Once when Miles was telling me how, when he grew up, he wanted to climb Mount Kilimanjaro,

I asked him how he got the idea. Maybe I imagined it, but Miles hesitated a beat. For an instant he looked almost scared. Then in a tone as close to contempt as a superpolite kid like Miles could allow himself, he said, "Oh, everybody knows that."

I've been using every excuse to ask Miles about school. Did you learn that at school? Did you do that at school? And Miles says yes or no, he did or he didn't, in that pure, sweet voice, as if he loved school and school loved him, and he's eager to go back in the fall. I'm not going to be the one to tell him the bad news. So all I can do is wait for Linda to figure the whole mess out. Apparently, she's written to Miles's school, but they just ignore her letters.

I've begun to feel as if Norris and Lucy are everywhere I look. Now I'm sure that the photo behind the photo, the one with the scratched-out faces, is a picture of them. I wonder which kid scratched them out. Or maybe it was Lucy, maybe she messed up the photo after Norris left the island. You always hear stories about people doing crazy stuff after they get dumped. . . . Didn't you tell me that Josh went off the deep end and got sent away to some rehab facility after you broke up?

I wonder if that book of poems in my room—*from Romeo to Juliet*—was a present from Norris to Lucy. One night, I took it out off the shelf and let it fall open because I figured that would be the page someone used to look at most. I read a poem I sort of remember studying in school, a poem in which some dude is trying to convince this girl to have sex with him because there's not a lot of time and they're not going to live forever. If it was a message from Norris to Lucy, he sure turned out to be right. They didn't have much time. I put the book back on my shelf.

Some kind of tension seems to be developing between me and the kids. But meanwhile I'm learning a lot about children. Like for example: kids know when you're trying to make them tell you something, especially when they don't want to. It's almost like a game they enjoy, as if they have something I want, and they're not going to give it up. Capture the flag or whatever.

The only way I've found to decrease the tension is to play games that are so wild, with so much running and yelling, that we lose ourselves and forget the other stuff. We forget to think at all, really. It's lucky the weather's been good and there's all this space to race around and make all the noise we want.

Yesterday, we played tag. I was "it," chasing Miles and Flora across the lawns behind the house. I can pretty much catch Miles without breaking a sweat, so I let him get a head start. But Flora can move fast when she wants to, so I have to work. Plus, being little, she can make these quick turns and twist out of my reach just when I think I have her.

We were having a good time, running and yelling at the top of our lungs. I was pretending to be a monster chasing them. For a moment I paused to catch my breath, but Miles and Flora kept racing as if I was right behind them.

I wish I could send you a picture of how gorgeous it was. The green lawn shone in the summer sun, the trees were leafy and fat and full and just starting to cast a few shadows.

I took off after the kids again, but slower, so I could enjoy the scenery.

I'd been thinking of a story my dad told me once. He was working on a house, pouring cement for a new foundation, and he suddenly got this funny feeling, this sense that something was there, this . . . presence. He heard a rattle and turned and saw a huge rattlesnake sitting on a rock nearby. I know there aren't supposed to be poisonous snakes around us, but there are a few here and there. Someone once told me a circus train dumped a carload of them in a wreck. My dad's point was that he got that weird feeling when you sense something before you see it. Like when that bat got into our house.

Which is a long way of saying that as the kids and I were playing tag on the lawn, I suddenly sensed someone there. Watching us. I looked up.

And I saw him, standing on a balcony encircling one of the towers that rose from the Black House.

It was the guy I'd seen at the library window. He was looking down at us. But not at *us*. He was staring at Miles. Once more I was sure I'd seen him before—I mean, before I saw him outside the library.

After a while the children noticed I'd stopped chasing them. I stared at the guy, long enough so that the children would see me and look in the same direction. I needed to know if they saw him, too. I wanted to know how they would react. They looked at me. They looked at the tower. They looked at me. They looked at the tower. Even from a distance, I could tell they didn't see him. Their little faces were puzzled as they came toward me.

Flora said, "Jack, what's the matter?"

Miles said, "What are you looking at?" For a fraction of a second, I could have sworn that he knew and was lying. Then I thought, No, he doesn't know. I'm being paranoid. Too much sun, too much running around. I needed a drink of water.

Suddenly, I felt weirdly faint, and bent over and grabbed my knees, the way Dad taught me to do if I got dizzy. When I looked up again, the man—or whatever he was—had vanished from the tower.

I couldn't imagine how he'd gotten down or,

for that matter, how he'd climbed up there. I told myself it was a trick of the light and the deepening shadows. But I knew what I'd seen, and I decided to tell Linda. Who's calling me right now. Got to run.

Love,

Jack

DEAR JACK,

I'm glad to hear that you're doing so well and have adjusted to the island and that you're even having fun. It's hard to believe that three weeks have passed since you left. Sometimes it seems like five minutes, and sometimes like five months. I miss you—even the loud music and the video games and all the stuff I used to complain about.

You know, Jack, something happened yesterday at work. I can't remember if I told you I got a couple of weeks of cabinet work in a house that this doctor from Boston is renovating. My friend Russ is doing the painting. I hadn't seen Russ for a while, and he asked how you were. I told him about your job on the island. . . . He got a strange look on his face and said he remembered reading about something strange that happened there, something nasty. Or maybe it was something that happened to some people *from* there. He thought maybe even a murder or a double murder. . . . I had to quit working for a minute and take a deep breath.

Russ always gets things wrong. He probably meant some other island completely. I figured you'd have heard about it by now, if there was anything . . . which I'm sure there isn't.

Anyhow, keep having fun. Say hello to the kids for me, even though I've never met them. Likewise Linda. I'm sure I'd like her as much as you say I would.

Love,
Your dad

DEAR DAD,

First of all, don't worry. I'm still having a nice time. I like the kids. I'll tell you more when I see you. Which won't be *all* that long. As for that story about the island . . . Russ did get it wrong. Or anyway, sort of wrong. There were two people who used to work here, then left and went someplace else, where they got into trouble and got shot or something . . . but they were losers to begin with. And they didn't get into real trouble until after they'd gone and no longer had anything to do with the island, which—believe me, Dad—is totally cool and safe.

I have to go now. Linda's calling me for dinner. She's made shepherd's pie, my favorite, with vegetables from the garden. You would like her garden, Dad, though I keep wondering what you would say about her using old golf clubs stuck in the ground to mark the rows.

Oh, and one more thing. Have you heard from Sophie or seen her or heard anything about her? I don't imagine you would. I know your paths never crossed except that one time when her car broke down and I needed you to pick us up. Wasn't that the first time you met?

But it's just that I was expecting a letter from her on the ferry that just came in, and there was no letter. So I was wondering. I'm sure I'll get a letter from her next time. But I was just wondering. Meanwhile, forget I asked.

Love,

Jack

DEAR SOPHIE,

Hi, remember me? Recognize the return address? Sophie, why haven't you written?

I keep thinking your letters must be getting lost somewhere. Otherwise I would have heard from you by now. You have to write to me. In a way, you could say I'm only here because of you, and I miss you, and when I don't hear from you . . . it makes me feel kind of crazy. Plus, out here on this island, there's not much to do except think and worry, and suddenly there's a lot to worry about. I worry about this ghost or whatever it is I've been seeing. Am I starting to lose my mind? I worry about Miles and Flora and what might have happened to them. I worry about everything they're not telling me.

Did I used to seem like a worried guy to you? I

never used to worry, though I had stuff to worry about. But now I worry about you and why you're not writing to me and whether you've forgotten me completely. So you know what? I think I'll just end the letter here and wait till I hear from you to write you another of those long letters where I tell you every little thing that's happened on this wacko island with these strange little kids . . . and maybe a ghost or two.

So, okay. It's your move. I'm waiting to hear from you. Good night till then.

Love you,

Jack

DEAR JACK,

I'm sorry if you were worried about me. And I'm sorry for not writing. Actually, I sort of thought I did write to you, and then I kind of remembered I didn't. I don't know how *that* happened.

Nothing much is going on here. But I've been kind of busy. I can't remember if I told you that Josh is back in town and that he came around the house to say hi the other day. Of course, it's completely over between us. He's so self-centered and snobby and full of himself. The minute I talk to him, I remember why we broke up! But it's nice to have an old friend around, someone I used to know so well. It helps distract me from missing you, which I really do.

Otherwise, I don't know what to say. . . . My job is boring. But I already told you that. I can't wait till you get back.

What's happening with you and the kids sounds exciting but also a little disturbing. Maybe you should tell Linda, who I feel I know, almost like a friend, just from reading your letters. What if this person you've been seeing is not a ghost but some-one who got on the island and is stalking the kids? How many movies like that have we seen? The creepy revenge murderer hiding in the woods out-side the lonely country house. And everyone knows who the psycho killer attacks first. It's always the babysitter!

Sorry, I don't mean to scare you, but I don't think

you should keep all this to yourself. It sounds to me like secrets have done enough damage on that island without you keeping another one. A big secret, and maybe a dangerous one, if the so-called ghost you've seen twice now—is it just twice?—turns out to be an ax murderer.

Don't keep it inside. That was always a problem of yours, keeping things bottled up. I remember how glad I was when you finally began to open up to me, because to tell the truth, you'd always scared me a little. Even though you talked a lot, you were so inward and intense, I was half afraid to find out who you really were. And then the person you turned out to be was so much kinder and sweeter than anyone I could have imagined. Tell someone, Jack. Please. Tell someone about the man you saw at the window and later on the tower.

I'd write more, but I've got to get ready. There's a party tonight on the beach, and even though I know it's going to be lonely without you, I've decided to go anyway, just to make myself get out of the house.

Write soon. Hugs,

Sophie

DEAR SOPHIE,

I was so glad to get your letter. I'm glad you're okay, and to tell you the truth, I'm glad that you miss me. And since I'm being honest, I have to tell you that it made me feel a little uncomfortable, your seeing Josh again. And your going to the beach party without me. But I believe you when you say he's just an old friend, and after all, you were the one who broke up with him, so there must have been a reason. Like you said.

I also decided to take your advice and tell Linda about this guy I'd been seeing hanging around the library and up on the tower. I've decided to tell her tonight, and all morning I've been thinking exactly how to put it so she won't think I'm crazy. Maybe the island does have a ghost. I can live with that. Especially if it turns out that I'm not the only person who's seen it. So what if I don't believe in ghosts? So what if you don't believe in ghosts? It happens that way all the time. Someone doesn't believe in ghosts, and then that person sees a ghost and starts to believe in ghosts.

Or maybe there was some perfectly reasonable explanation for my . . . hallucination. Once when I was little my dad took me to this place called Mystery Hill. You drive up a hill, but the funny thing is, you feel like you're driving down a hill. Maybe this was something like that. Or maybe you're right, maybe it was an actual person, in which case Linda and I and the kids ought to leave the island on the next ferry and send the police back to find him.

Anyway, like I said, I was thinking how to tell Linda. I was going to tell her last night after dinner when she and I sat on the porch.

But in the meantime, yesterday, before I could say anything, another strange thing happened.

It was just after lunch. Miles was reading a book about the first organized expedition to the South Pole. He said he couldn't put it down and he wanted to spend the afternoon in his room reading. Linda and I looked at each other. I could tell we were both thinking the same thing: What a good reader Miles was, a good kid, and probably a good student. So what had he done to get himself expelled?

Honestly, I can't believe it's taking Linda so long to deal with this. Because sooner or later she has to tell Miles and the children's uncle, and something will have to be worked out about school. They'll have to face what Miles did or what the school says he did. But I guess Linda has been through enough rough patches with the kids, so I can understand her wanting to keep things calm and peaceful—which they are, Sophie!—for as long as she can. Also it makes me even more reluctant to bother her with the crazy idea that I might have seen a ghost. Linda has enough problems. I told myself I should probably solve this mystery on my own.

Since Miles was busy reading, I asked Flora what she wanted to do, and she said she wanted to take a plant walk. I said that was fine with me.

I always like our plant walks. I know it sounds

corny, but Flora is like a little butterfly, and it's enjoyable to walk behind the butterfly skipping from flower to flower. Except that this little butterfly has a serious knowledge of botany. This butterfly knows the Latin names for everything that grows around here.

Every time we go out, Flora makes a bouquet of all the wildflowers she finds. They're always straggly, scrawny collections of buds and blossoms, and to tell the truth, I sometimes wonder why a kid who supposedly loves plants so much would want to tear their heads off and bunch them together and bring them back to the house, where she leaves them around so we're always finding them in the most unexpected places. On the toilet tank in the downstairs bathroom, on the windowsill in the library.

Once we came to breakfast and discovered one of her creations sprouting from the sugar bowl. She hadn't thought to dump out the sugar before she added water for her flowers, so by the time Linda found them, they were wilting in several inches of syrupy sludge. Flora always gets upset when Linda throws her bouquets out, so Linda waits until they're pretty far over the edge into smelly, limp vegetation, and then she discreetly tosses them away.

Anyhow, that's what Flora was doing on this perfect day I was describing: making one of her flower collections to bring inside. She was wearing a bright orange T-shirt and orange shorts—with a butterfly print, believe it or not—and she looked like a monarch fluttering, running ahead, calling me to follow. She's always so proud of herself when she knows a Latin name, and since I don't, I can only smile encouragingly and say how amazing it is that a girl her age can rattle off eight-syllable, three-word names for every weed and every rush that grows by the side of the lake.

That's what we were doing, walking around the lake. Flora was shouting the Latin names, and I was smiling and being impressed.

Then I looked across the lake.

A woman was standing near the boathouse, staring at us from the other shore. But she was really looking at Flora, just like the man on the tower had been looking at Miles.

Though the weather was warm, she was wearing a long black dress beneath a hooded cloak. She was hugging herself, and she looked cold. Beneath the hood, her face was pale, and even from a distance I could tell that she was unhappy. And she was beautiful.

The hood slipped down to her shoulders. I saw that her hair was red. And suddenly I knew where I'd seen her before. On the ferry to the island. She was the one who'd been weeping on deck, the one who came downstairs and played cards with the older guy.

And now I knew where I'd seen him. First on the ferry and then at the library window. Standing in the tower. Could the couple have gotten off behind me and sneaked onto the island? Or returned to the island on the next ferry for some mysterious purpose of their own?

The beautiful red-haired woman remained there, staring at Flora.

Flora didn't notice. She kept running from plant to plant as if she were visiting old friends. She acted as if we were the only ones there. As if she was the only person there—just Flora and the plants.

I opened my mouth to yell at the woman, to ask her what she was doing on private property. Then I stopped. I needed to know if Flora saw what I saw.

I said, "Flora, what's the pretty flower over there? Between the edge of the lake and the boathouse?" I pointed toward the woman. The woman saw me point. She looked at me, questioningly, but only for a moment. Then she looked back at Flora.

The woman didn't care if I was pointing. She looked through me, just as she had on the deck of the ferry. How had she gotten here, and what did she want from me and the children? Of course I thought of Norris and Lucy. I had to find out what they looked like.

All this seemed to take forever. But I don't think more than a minute passed before Flora said to me, "What flower? I don't see any flowers between the shore and the boathouse."

"What do you see?" I asked.

"The lawn," she said. "Green grass." She told me the Latin name for grass.

I watched her for some sign that she was lying. But it just didn't seem possible that this little girl could be that good an actress, that excellent a liar. I couldn't believe she could see the redheaded woman across the lake and convince me she'd seen nothing at all.

"Nothing else?" I said. "No one?"

"Nothing," she said. "No one? Who would be there?"

When I looked again there was no one there. The woman had vanished. I felt as if I had lost something.

"What's wrong?" said Flora. She was still slightly out of breath from running, and her little face was flushed and open and expectant.

"Nothing," I said. "I think I'm seeing things."

"Poor Jack," said Flora. "It must be the sun. Let's get you inside and get you something to drink."

It felt wrong, being taken care of by the child I was supposed to be taking care of. We went back to the kitchen. I hoped Linda wasn't there. I was afraid she'd see on my face everything that had happened. That is, if I knew what had happened. I worried she'd take one look at me and see a guy who'd hallucinated a woman staring at Flora from the far shore of the lake, the woman I'd seen playing cards on the ferry from the mainland, the woman who got killed after a card game.

Linda was in the garden, kneeling down among the tall plants and the golf clubs. Flora poured me some ice tea and gave me a sugar cookie, baked by Linda.

"Eat this," she said. "It'll help you get your strength back." Flora nibbled on one herself. I told myself: No kid sees a ghost and starts nibbling a cookie like nothing happened.

I said, "Flora, I was just wondering . . . do you have any pictures of Lucy and Norris?"

Flora flinched, as if I'd struck her. It crossed my

mind that the kids and I had never once spoken the names of the people who used to work here, the people who left and were killed.

"How do you know about them?" Flora said.

"Linda told me," I said. "Of course."

Flora didn't ask any more. It seemed she didn't want to know what I knew, and she didn't want me to ask her anything else.

"Do you?" I said. "Do you have any pictures?"

This time I could see Flora trying to lie, but it just wasn't in her. If she said there was no woman on the opposite shore, it meant she hadn't seen her. It meant something was seriously wrong with me. But no. I felt okay. Sort of. I just had to find out the truth, and everything would make sense and be fine.

Flora said, "Promise you won't tell Miles?" Did that mean she had a picture of Norris and Lucy?

It was the first time that either of them had suggested I keep something secret from the other. I promised not to say a word.

Well, Sophie, I'm stopping here. That's all I'm going to say for now. If you want to know how the story comes out, you'll have to write me another letter.

Love, I guess,

Jack

DEAR JACK,

I sat down and wrote you the minute I got your letter. I want to hear what happens; I want to know if Flora had a picture and if she showed it to you and what you saw. So I'm writing you right away, even though I don't have much to say.

I went to that party I mentioned, and just like I expected, it was boring. Josh was there, so we talked about how we used to be together and obviously weren't right for each other. I told him how close you and I are and how well we get along. Doesn't that make you feel better?

Listen, I've got to go now. Some kids are outside waiting for me to go swim in the river. But I promised I would write if I wanted you to tell me more, so okay, now I've written. And you promised to go on with the story.

Miss you.

S

DEAR SOPHIE,

I can't help wishing your letter had been a little longer. I can't help feeling like you wrote it on your way out the door, maybe because you said you wrote it on your way out the door. Maybe next time you'll write me a few more lines. Like maybe another paragraph. But okay, a deal's a deal. I told you I'd go on with the story if you wrote back, so here it goes:

When I asked Flora if she had a picture of Lucy and Norris, she told me to come with her, and we went to her room. Miles's door was shut, but still Flora walked on tiptoe and put her finger to her lips. This was going to be—this had to be—top secret.

Flora shut her door, went to her bureau, and

opened the drawer where she keeps her socks. They were so tiny, like doll socks, it broke my heart. I'd never realized how small her feet were until I saw those tiny socks. Anyway, she reached under the neat little stacks of socks and took out two photographs. She didn't show me the first one, which she immediately put away again, but even from a distance I could tell that it was a print of the portrait downstairs—her mom and dad together with her mother's family in India.

Then she held out the other photo and shut her eyes as if she couldn't stand to look at it. I wondered why she'd agreed to show it to me. What did she want me to know? How much would she tell me now that her brother wasn't around? And I thought how pleased Linda would be, what a great job she would think I was doing, if I found out something from Flora that Linda didn't know.

I looked at the photo—another print of the one I'd found in the library. The one with the faces scratched out. But in this one the faces were undamaged, and they stared out of the picture at me.

In the photo a woman and a man stood arm in arm on the lakeshore, with Miles and Flora, by the boathouse—exactly where the redheaded woman stood today. The man was the one I'd seen at the library window, and the woman was the same one I'd seen at the lake.

It was the couple I'd seen playing cards on the boat.

"Who are they?" I said, though I knew. I knew.

Flora's smile was chilly. "You know who they are, silly. That's Lucy. Norris and Lucy."

There were dozens of questions I should have asked. What did you do with Norris and Lucy? What did they do to you? Did you like them? Do you miss them? But suddenly I was too scared. I couldn't have said what frightened me, but I was shaking. But why? Lucy and Norris were dead. They couldn't be here on the island. There had to be another explanation for the weird things that had been happening.

Suddenly, I couldn't stand there anymore, looking at their faces, at smug little Flora looking at me.

I said, "They look nice, Flora. They look like very nice people. I guess you learned a lot from them. But you know what? I'm really tired. I need to go take a nap."

I hurried off to my room and fell on my bed. But I couldn't sleep. I kept thinking about the photo and about the couple I'd seen on the boat. And about what Linda had told me. Something didn't add up. If Lucy and Norris were dead, I couldn't have seen them. But if they were alive, what were they doing on the island, and why didn't the children see them? Were they all playing some crazy mind game with me?

I was curious to find out if, at dinner, Flora would give any sign that she'd shown me the photo. I wondered if she regretted it, or if she was afraid I'd mention it or that Miles might find out. But she was as lighthearted and chatty as ever. Her dark eyes were trusting and innocent. She didn't seem like someone who'd just given up a secret. What she'd shown me that afternoon was just a photo of a teacher and a handyman who used to work here.

But I knew it was more than a photo. It was the first turning of the key that might unlock a chest that I wasn't sure I wanted to open.

Linda had made a delicious salad with tuna, olives, ham, and hardboiled eggs. But I wasn't hungry. I chewed every mouthful for a long time, so it would look like I was eating.

Somehow I got through the meal and helped Linda clean up. I said good night to the children. Somehow I kept myself from blurting out what I had to say until Linda and I were sitting on the porch with our pot of chamomile tea.

I said, "I need to tell you something. Something strange." I told myself to keep calm. The story I had to tell was so peculiar that I had to be very reasonable and clear.

I told Linda everything: how I'd seen the couple on the boat, and then the man at the library window, and in the tower, and then the scratched-out photo, and the woman on the lakeshore, and then the picture of Norris and Lucy.

"Where did you find the photo?" Linda said.

"In a book," I answered. I thought it would be okay to keep back one little detail. If I confessed that Flora had shown it to me, and Linda mentioned it to Flora, the little girl would never trust me again.

Linda sighed and stared out at the night. On the lawns the lightning bugs were putting on their shooting-star show.

Finally she said, "It's something that happens, Jack. Welcome to adult life. Remember that movie where the guy says, 'I see dead people'?"

"The one with Bruce Willis?" I said. "Sure."

"Well," said Linda, "the truth is, everyone sees dead people. Often I see a shadow at the edge of my field of vision, and I'm sure it's Lucy or Norris, though I know it couldn't be. I think I see my husband coming out to the garden, the way he used to when he was well. Every time I go to the mainland, I imagine I see him walking down the street. But guess what? It's not him. No matter how much I want it to be him. Death doesn't mean they've left your mind, and your mind sends messages to your eyes that sometimes have nothing to do with what you actually see. Do you ever think you see your mom?"

"Not really," I said. "I don't remember her that well." I had the feeling that Linda was talking to herself. Because if she thought about it a minute, she'd realize I'd never seen Norris and Lucy alive, so how could I be seeing them now? And how could I have seen them on the ferry on my way here, before I'd ever heard of them? And I was getting tired of her always talking about her dead husband.

Linda sighed. "I don't know what you saw, Jack, or what you think you saw. But you didn't see them. Norris and Lucy are dead. I promise you. I had to go to the mainland and identify their bodies. It was not a pleasant job. I haven't forgotten. They were dead. You didn't see them here."

"So are you saying I saw their ghosts?"

"There are no ghosts," said Linda. "Just people's imaginations, and you obviously have a vivid one. Who knows what vibes you're picking up, what you're getting from the kids? Haven't you and someone else—someone you're close to—ever thought exactly the same thing at the same moment? It used to happen with me and my husband all the time. Sometimes we'd wake up in the morning and find out we'd dreamed . . . well, not exactly the same dream, but dreams with the same things in them. Maybe you're psychic, Jack. Stranger things happen, believe me."

Linda's voice faded away, and I thought of how once you and I fell asleep on the beach. And when we woke up, we'd both dreamed about schools. Schools of fish. But your school was full of crustaceans, and mine of baby starfish. Remember how weird that was, and how happy it made us?

Maybe I am psychic. Which would mean you'd better be careful, Sophie. Be careful what you do and say and who you hang out with. Because I'm going to know. Meanwhile,

Love from your psychic boyfriend,

Jack

DEAR SOPHIE,

It's been another long time without a letter from you. I've started to get that uneasy feeling I get when you don't write.

I'm not trying to guilt you, Sophie. But the truth is, I haven't been feeling all that well lately. It's not exactly physical. More mental, in a way. I'm edgy, but it's more than that. I feel as if the colors of everything have gotten a little brighter, and sounds a little louder, and when the kids speak to me, their voices have a tinny echo, like I'm hearing them from the far end of a tunnel or over a bad phone connection.

It doesn't happen all the time. I have these little spells, and then they pass, and I'm normal again. Do you think I could have something wrong with my brain? My mom died young when something went wrong with her brain. . . . Well, I'm not going to think about that now.

Otherwise I've been fine. And it's mostly been quiet here. Miles finished reading his book on Antarctica and started one about the North Pole.

Flora never mentioned showing me the photo of Norris and Lucy. She and I have been playing tennis and collecting tadpoles and throwing them back in the lake. I haven't seen any ghosts, so maybe that's all over. Maybe I was getting sick, and now this weird brain thing means I've got some kind of virus, and now it will get better.

Like I said, I've been fine.

That is, until last night.

I wish I could remember what I was dreaming when I woke up. Because I had that feeling that waking up was part of the dream, or as if waking up was the answer to a question the dream was asking. I wish I could remember what made me get out of bed and go to the window.

Maybe it was the full moon. It was so blindingly bright that the lawn outside the house seemed as if it was illuminated by stadium lights.

I sensed something moving on the lawn before I saw what it was.

It was Flora in her white nightdress, gliding across

the wet grass. She was heading for the lake, and she seemed to be staring at the other shore—at the place where I'd seen the redheaded woman I still can't bring myself to call Lucy. Something about Flora's posture made her look as if she'd heard her name called and was answering the call.

"Linda," I shouted. "Flora's outside." I threw on my clothes and ran out. Linda appeared from her wing of the house, running right behind me. Linda grabbed Flora, who started screaming. Linda hugged her and held her tight.

I can still hear Flora crying with terror. But of course she was frightened. We'd scared her.

"Where am I?" Flora said.

"You're outside," I said. "You're fine."

"You're with us. We're right here." Linda gathered Flora up in her arms and slung her over her shoulder.

I asked, "Do you want me to take her?"

"Flora's a feather," Linda said, and we turned back toward the house.

Miles was standing in the doorway, watching us, his eyes as cold as the stars in the sky above us.

Okay, enough for now. I need to get some sleep. I'm starting to feel light-headed. Did I mention I haven't been sleeping well? I don't know what to do. Maybe I'll just lie here with my eyes closed and think about you and wonder what you're doing.

Love,

Jack

DEAR DAD,

I had a little virus or something, but I think it's gone now. I didn't want to worry you. That's why I didn't mention it. But like I said, everything's cool. The summer's rushing by, and to tell you the truth, I'm counting the days till I get home. But I'm fine. Don't worry about me. I'll write more soon. By the way, you never mentioned if you've seen Sophie. Let me know.

Love,

Jack

DEAR JACK,

I'm glad you're feeling better, but I wish you'd

told me you weren't well. I'd rather hear everything that's happening with you, even if there's a problem. Especially when there's a problem. And you hadn't written for a while, so I was getting concerned. So I was happy to hear you're okay.

Oh, I forgot to tell you. I did see Sophie. Last week. I'd been working hard all day, and the doctor whose cabinets I'm building had been giving me a hard time. So to make myself feel better, I stopped off for ice cream on the way home.

A car full of kids was parked outside the ice cream place, all laughing and having a good time. I thought I saw Sophie in the front seat, next to some guy. I almost felt like she saw me and recognized me and didn't want me to notice her.

But when she could tell I'd seen her, she got out of the car and came over and said hello. She asked me how you were and told me to say hello to you and to give you her love. It seemed a little strange to me that she was asking me how you were. I figured you must be writing to her more than you write to me. But what do I know about kids today?

Maybe you're practicing telepathy or something. Or maybe she's gotten a million letters from you, and she didn't want me to feel left out.

She told me the kids in the car were her cousins. Which is why I'm telling you. Otherwise I might not have mentioned the whole thing.

Anyhow, she sends her love. And so do I.

Your dad

DEAR JACK,

Are you sure you're okay? If you're not feeling well, you should tell someone. I have to go now, but I'm worried about you. Write me soon.

Love,

Sophie

DEAR SOPHIE,

Nice of you to write, even if it was about fifteen words. Nice of you to be so concerned.

Actually, I've been okay. But things haven't gotten any less bizarre.

After Flora's little sleepwalking incident—that's

what Linda and I decided it probably was—Linda thought it would be a good idea to take her to see a doctor on the mainland. She was sure there was nothing wrong, but she wanted to get it checked out. Linda asked if I was okay with staying on the island with Miles overnight.

I said I was, though in fact it made me jumpy. The last time Linda left me alone, just for the day, was when Norris's ghost appeared for the first time. And now, all those visitations later, who knew what would happen if Linda left for a whole day and night?

On the other hand, there were no ghosts. It was only me and Miles. Lately he's been pretty low maintenance, reading his exploration books and putting down the book only when I make him come outside for tennis or a boat ride. I tell him that his uncle isn't paying me for him to read exactly what he'd be reading if I weren't there.

On the day that Linda and Flora left there was nothing to do *but* read. The sky was dark and cloudy, and by the time I woke up, I could hear a steady soaking rain pounding on the roof. At breakfast I asked Linda if she was sure she wanted to go on such a nasty day, and Linda said it was better that way. She and Flora would get everything checked out—she smiled at Flora to make sure she understood this was all routine and wasn't going to hurt and was nothing to be scared of—and they could save the beautiful days for playing outside and being in the garden.

I'd told my dad I planned to read a lot when I was on the island, but I hadn't kept my promise. I've been playing with my secret collection of video games, probably more than I should have—mostly in the late afternoons and early evenings, when the children are watching Linda cook and I'm waiting to be called downstairs for dinner.

So this seemed like a good day for me to catch up on my reading, though this time I certainly wasn't going to do it in the library.

After Miles and I waved to Linda and Flora and watched the red truck disappear down the road, Miles asked—very politely, of course—if it would

if he went to his room. He said he was
iddle of a book by an explorer who lived
he Marsh Arabs in what's now Iraq. I said
that sounded interesting, though I didn't think it
did.

I went to my room. I felt a little guilty that this
kid was reading his way through all the books in
the house and I was playing Grand Theft Auto. I
looked through my books again, and guess what I
found? A collection of famous ghost stories. I read
one story called "The Monkey's Paw" and another
in which a girl sees dead people pass by a window
while she's having tea with an elderly relative. By
the time I'd started the third story—about a haunted
dollhouse—I wanted company, and I decided to go
look for Miles.

I knocked on Miles's door, but no one answered. I
found him lying on top of his bed, so involved in his
book that he hadn't heard me push open the door.

"Hey," I said. "Want to play a video game?"

He couldn't have looked more shocked if I'd said,
Want to jump off the roof and learn how to fly?

Want to catch a toad in the garden and eat it? Want to learn the secret of the universe? For a moment I wondered if he'd ever heard of video games. But he'd been to school. He probably knew all about video games.

Miles broke into a wide grin, which quickly faded. He actually looked around to make sure that no one was listening. Then he said, "Cool. That would be cool."

Miles and I went up to my room and sat down in front of the console. I thought Grand Theft Auto might be a little much for him. So I got this Wild West game that I'd loved when I was younger and I'd sort of grown out of. But I liked having it with me, so I'd brought it along.

I showed Miles how to play, and he caught on fast. Naturally there were video games—against the rules or not—at his school. He went first, and he was the sheriff, walking down the streets of this frontier town, blowing away the desperadoes who jumped off the roofs or fired at him from the doorways. I coached him a little, telling him when to shoot and jump and dodge, and he was doing pretty well.

That was when I began to notice a strange thing.

Among the bad guys he had to kill were a couple of characters I'd never seen in the game before. I got closer and looked over Miles's shoulder so I could be sure I wasn't mistaken. But I wasn't wrong. I wasn't imagining things. I only wish I were.

Two of the characters that kept reappearing and threatening him with guns and bombs and bows and arrows were cartoon versions of Norris and Lucy. They shot at him from the alleys and windows, and Miles shot them dead. Did he know that's what he was doing? Did he see who they were? Or was I hallucinating again? Were the villains the same Wild West bad guys as always, or had Norris and Lucy somehow found their way into the game— the same way they'd found their way onto the boat and to the library, the tower, and the lakeshore?

Miles asked if I wanted to play. I said I was a little tired; I hadn't slept well last night. I said I'd just lie down on the bed. He could play as long as he wanted.

I must have fallen asleep. When I awoke, Miles was gone. The room was empty. The video console was dark. It was still raining hard outside, and I had a fever.

The next thing I knew, Linda was leaning over me, her cool hand on my forehead. I was sick, but not too out of it to feel grateful that Linda wasn't asking about the forbidden video console in my room.

"I think I'm sick," I said.

"Good diagnosis, Dr. Jack," said Linda. "There's something going around. Actually, the doctor said that he thought Flora might have had a little bug or something. He thought that might have been what disturbed her sleep and made her wander outside in the dark. Maybe you caught it from her, though heaven knows how either of you could have been exposed to germs, given how isolated we are on this island. Maybe Flora caught it from a bumble-bee and passed it on to you."

The ghosts made us sick, I thought. But I knew if I said that, it would be the fever talking.

"So here's my plan," said Linda. "Let's sit tight and not panic. Let's keep you warm and full of fluids and see if your fever goes down."

That sounds like a good plan to me, I wanted to say. But what I heard come out was "Plan . . . me."

"I knew you'd agree," said Linda. "Don't tell Jim Crackstone I said so, but this is one of those times when television would really come in handy. I remember when I was a kid, I loved staying home sick from school and getting to watch TV all day."

"Tell me about it," I said.

"See?" said Linda. "You sound better already."

For what was left of the day, and into the evening, Linda was in and out of my room, bringing me water and tea, covering me with more blankets. At one point she put a cool cloth on my head, and it felt so good, I almost did something intensely embarrassing. I almost grabbed her hand and kissed it. I kept thinking how much I wished she was my mom, and I promised myself that when I got better and went home, I would make sure, no matter what

it took, that Linda and my dad met and fell in love
and got married.

I'd completely lost track of time, but I know that
it was late at night when Linda came into my room
one last time with one more glass of water with
lemon and two more pills to bring down my fever.

I said, "Couldn't you stay here for a while? There's
that couch . . ."

Linda said, "You're a big boy, Jack. And you've just
got the flu. You're not dying. Trust me, I'll come
check on you a couple of times during the night."

So that's what I thought was happening when I
woke up . . . who knows how many hours later. I
thought Linda was looking in on me.

My fever had come roaring back. I was freezing
and burning, both at once. Everything hurt. My
head, my throat, my legs. Every hair felt like a nee-
dle of pain sticking into my scalp. Even the backs of
my hands ached.

I felt the pressure of someone sitting at the end of
my bed. Thank God Linda had come.

"Linda," I said. "Linda?"

A voice, a woman's voice, said, "Thank you for letting me in."

Are you reading this, Sophie? Have you actually made it to the end of this letter? Well, I'm glad to hear it.

You know what makes me mad, Sophie? The idea of you holding this letter in one hand and reading it with one eye while you're looking in the mirror and brushing mascara on the other. So you can hurry up and go out with your friends. Friends? With your old friend Josh. Do you think I don't know that my dad saw you outside the ice cream stand, and do you think my dad didn't know that Josh was sitting next to you in the front seat of the car?

So what are you thinking, Sophie? Gee, I'm glad I didn't have to take care of boring old Jack when he was sick with the flu. Or maybe you're wondering if the person sitting on my bed scared me to death or bit me and now I'm a vampire, too.

Nothing like that happened, obviously. But a lot

of other strange stuff happened, things so bizarre that I don't feel like the same person I used to be. The Jack you knew has left the building. You can call me New Jack. And New Jack is not going to write you another line, he's not going to tell you what happened next, unless you tell Josh to drop dead and you write me a letter this minute.

Love,

Your boyfriend,

New Jack

DEAR JACK,

Your letter really upset me. I was relieved to know you hadn't gotten worse, since obviously you wouldn't be writing to me if you hadn't recovered. But your tone was so different, as if you really had become another person. Are you sure you're okay? Does your dad know what's happening? Don't you think someone should tell him?

And why are you being so mean to me? I'm not going out with Josh. Where did you get the idea that your dad saw me with him? The afternoon I ran into your dad outside the ice cream stand, I was with my cousins. That was my cousin Biff beside me in the front seat. You can ask anyone. Ask my mom and dad if you don't believe me. I never lied to you, Jack.

I assume that by the time you get this you'll be completely better and back to the nice, sweet person I knew before you went to that island. I could kill my dad for setting this whole thing up. Anyhow, it's not that long now until you return. Only another three weeks and you'll be home, and we'll be back together and you can see for yourself who I really care about—you or Josh.

So anyway, keep writing to me. I want to know what happened next and who was sitting on your bed that night you had the fever.

Love,

Sophie

DEAR SOPHIE,

Well, that certainly speeded things up! I guess the only way to get you to write back without waiting a million years is for me to be dying of fever with a ghost in my room.

Because, Sophie, you know who was at the end of my bed. You know it was Lucy. When I heard her voice, it sounded so familiar. As if it were a voice I'd been hearing inside my head from before I can remember.

"It's cold in here," she said.

"I know. I'm freezing," I said.

"But you're sick," she said. "I'm just dead."

"You're dead?" I said.

"You already knew that," she said.

"I am seriously sick," I said. "Is this really happening?"

"This is really happening," she said.

Once she said that, a lot of things seemed settled. Since she was dead, I didn't need to ask her how she'd gotten on the ferry or on the other side of the lake or, for that matter, how she got into my room. Though why had she thanked me for letting her in? My head was buzzing with fever.

"I saw you on the boat," I said.

"I know. I saw you, too. But I didn't know who you were then or where you were going. Despite what the living think, ghosts don't know everything. We know almost everything. But not some things."

"That's kind of confusing," I said.

"I'm sorry," she said. "You have to be one of us to understand." I wondered who she meant by us. Her and Norris? Or all the restless ghosts that still wandered among the living?

"Why were you on the boat?"

"Because I wanted to see the island again? Because I was happy here? Because I cared about the children? All those reasons and more. And Norris wouldn't let me go without him, so . . ."

Did I say that Lucy talked very fast, almost double normal speed? Maybe that was where I got the impression that she wasn't sure how long she could stay. It reinforced my sense that she was there—and not there. I felt her weight on the edge of my bed, the weight of an actual body, but at the same time I could see through her. I could see the wall of my room through her red hair and through the golden aura around her. She seemed nervous and ready to vanish if anyone saw her or scared her or told her to leave. Strangely, I didn't want her to leave.

Maybe because I was sure she would stay only for a while, I said, "Did you do something bad to the children?" I would have waited longer to ask something like that if I thought we had more time. And I would never have asked a living person so directly.

"It wasn't good," said Lucy. "What we did wasn't good."

"You and Norris?"

Lucy jumped when I said his name, then nodded. Or I think she nodded. A cold wind blew through the room. It was as if it was suddenly winter and someone had opened a window.

I couldn't bring myself to ask her what they'd done.

I said, "I saw you playing cards on the boat."

"The cards?" she said. "You saw the cards? I wish you hadn't. That was the worst part, really."

"The worst part? How bad could cards be?" It

was bizarre how much better I felt, talking to a ghost. At the same time, I was thinking that I must be getting worse, and that my rising fever was the reason I imagined I was having a conversation with a dead person.

"It was what we were playing for," she said.

"High stakes?"

"Nothing higher," said Lucy. Somehow in my delirium I remembered Linda saying that Norris and Lucy hadn't been interested in the children's bodies, but their souls.

Actually, I was hearing Linda's voice—asking how I felt and if I needed more water.

"I'm sleeping," I said. "I'm fine." I was afraid that Linda had scared the ghost away. What if I never got to hear what was so terrible about a game of cards?

"You're not fine," Linda said. "You're burning up. I'm going to get more ibuprofen. I'll be back in a minute."

Only after I heard Linda's footsteps going down the stairs did Lucy materialize again. Not that she'd been gone. She knew that Linda was there, and she'd heard what Linda had said. She knew we didn't have much time. I wondered why it mattered, why a ghost couldn't just reappear whenever she wanted.

She said, "Do you know what strip poker is?"

Well, this was a pretty crazy discussion to be having with a ghost! I nodded. Remember that second cousin of yours that was there for the weekend last summer, and every time things got quiet, he'd say, "Who wants to play strip poker?" And no one did. Dear God, I prayed, don't let Lucy and Norris have played strip poker with Miles and Flora.

"It was Norris's game," said Lucy. "It was always Norris's game. And the thing about Norris was, just the way he told you the rules made you realize there was no hope: you were going to lose. It was like strip poker except that none of the players took their clothes off. It was more like some kind of psychic strip poker and Truth or Dare combined. Every time you lost, and you always lost, you had to give up some terrible secret, some horrible truth about yourself that you'd never told anyone before.

In case you hesitated or forgot, Norris had questions. What was the worst thing you ever did? The stupidest thing you ever said? The cruelest thought you ever had? The worst lie you ever told? The nastiest lie a person ever told about you? The meanest thing someone ever said about you that you knew was true?

"If you lied, if you made something up, Norris would know it. And he would start shouting at you until you told the truth. Every time you lost a hand, which was every time you played, he'd repeat all the other previous secrets you'd told about yourself. So you had to listen to them over and over. Like one of those children's songs that keep growing, 'Old MacDonald' or 'The Twelve Days of Christmas.' But hurtful and wicked and evil. You hated yourself when those games were through. You wanted to crawl away and disappear. You would have died if you could—"

I wondered what Lucy had been forced to admit about herself. What awful secrets had made her cry on the boat in that heartsick way? But before I could imagine how to begin to ask, I heard Linda's footsteps returning.

I said, "Did you and Norris ever play that game with the children?"

Lucy said, "We did. That was the worst of the worst. At first they thought it might be fun, playing cards with the grown-ups. And by the time they realized what the game was, Norris wouldn't let them quit. It was terrible for them. They hated it. It always made them cry. Flora and Miles would be weeping and weeping. But they kept playing. Mostly children aren't old enough to have done anything bad, especially not those kids. But all little children secretly believe they're sinners. Especially those kids. Everything that Miles and Flora said seemed like some wrenching confession extracted under torture, and I could tell they were thinking about what they'd said even when we weren't playing.

"Eventually I began to suspect that Miles and Flora were making things up for the game. Confessing bad things they'd done to their parents, though, from what I understood, they were so young when their parents were killed, they couldn't possibly have done any of the things they said. But I think that they began to believe the stories they were telling. And those two innocent little children started to imagine that they were truly evil deep down in their souls—"

Evil was the word that Miles's school had used in the letter explaining why they didn't want him back. . . .

My bedroom light flashed on. The brightness was so painful, I felt as if a rocket had exploded behind each of my eyes.

"Here are the pills," said Linda.

"Thanks a lot," I said. "I was sleeping." I was lying. I couldn't bear that Linda had scared Lucy away.

"You sound annoyed," said Linda. "You must be feeling better."

"Well, I don't," I said. "I feel worse."

"Hey, what's that smell?" Linda said.

"What smell?" I asked. But I knew, because I could smell it, too.

"Shalimar hand cream," said Linda. "I haven't smelled that since—"

"Since Lucy left?" I said.

"How do you know? I can't remember telling you that."

"You did." I was lying, but I had no choice. I wanted her to leave so maybe Lucy would come back.

"Great," Linda said. "I must be getting sick, too. I've gone straight from 98.6 to some kind of fever dream."

"You get some rest," I said. "Take some of those pills you brought me."

"I think I will," said Linda. "Promise you'll call if you need me."

"I promise," I told Linda. "We'll both feel better in the morning."

That's all for now, Sophie.

Love,

Jack

DEAR DAD,

Well, I really came down with a bad flu this time. I know I said I'd tell you, but I didn't want to scare you. I was too sick to write. Obviously, I'm better now. But my mood's been kind of strange. I guess the island is finally getting to me. Especially now that I'm past the halfway mark. I'll be really glad to see you. By the way, have you seen Sophie? I got two letters from her in a row, and then after that nothing, and it's kind of freaking me out.

Let me know if you see her or if you hear anything.

Lots of love,

Jack

DEAR SOPHIE,

I guess what all this means is, we should probably break up. I know this might come as a shock to you. But it only seems right. After all, you didn't fool me for a minute when you kept saying you're seeing Josh again—and that you're just friends. Did you think I didn't notice your letters were getting further and further apart and less and less affectionate?

Did you think I couldn't tell that you had to force yourself to write to me, probably only because you felt guilty? Did you think it didn't get my attention when you kept mentioning Josh's name, because you couldn't help it, even when you were trying not to?

But in a way it's all okay. All for the best, as they say. Because now I don't have to feel guilty about the fact that I seem to have fallen in love with a ghost.

I know you were probably expecting this. I know you probably saw it coming the minute I described seeing Lucy on the deck of the ferry. Remember? I knew what you were thinking. Or I used to know. I knew what you'd say about the seagull warning me, the seagull who called Lucy's name in my dream. But I was never as smart as you, Sophie. We both knew that from the beginning. Even if I worked all summer on this miserable island taking care of two weird kids, even if I made enough money, I was never going to get into the same college as you did. So that was always a joke. We were always going to break up. So why not do it sooner rather than later?

So, okay, now that it looks like we've broken up, I'll admit it. When I woke up the next morning, I was feeling a lot better. Except that I couldn't stop thinking of Lucy. I got out of bed and searched my room. But of course she wasn't there. She wasn't anywhere. She's dead. It's not like I don't know how totally strange this is. It's one thing to be in love with an older woman. But it's something else completely to be in love with a ghost.

I almost feel like at some point I split into two people. One of them is suffering about this. And the other me can joke about it and think, Hey, what's the problem? The joking me says, Come on, Jack. What kind of future do you think you'll have with this person? I mean, this ghost.

But then the suffering me goes back to bed and closes his eyes and hopes he'll dream about Lucy. The heartbroken me goes to the window and looks out toward the lake and prays and prays to see her standing near the boathouse. The lovesick me wishes I could get sick again and run a high fever so she would come visit me and thank me for letting her in. Am I hurting your feelings, Sophie? Somehow, I doubt it. You've got Josh now. But since the only thing about me that interested you was my story, I'll give you a thrill and tell you more. Remember, you asked for it.

I couldn't believe I'd been frightened when I'd gone to the lake with Flora and seen Lucy on the opposite shore. If I'd known what I know now, I would have just left Flora there, showing off, calling out the Latin names of all her stupid plants. I would have run around to the other side of the lake and begged Lucy not to leave.

Why hadn't I pleaded with Lucy to stay last night? She'd left when Linda came upstairs. It was all Linda's fault. Then I wondered if Norris knew that Lucy had come to see me and if he was the one she was scared of, not Linda. Maybe he was waiting for her somewhere, maybe that was the reason she had to rush off.

I fell into a feverish sleep as soon as I took the pills Linda brought. Maybe I was even asleep before

Linda left. If only I could have stayed awake and found Lucy again. But I couldn't. I didn't.

I opened my eyes.

It was morning.

I went downstairs to the kitchen, where Linda and the kids were eating breakfast.

"Miracle cure!" said Linda.

"There wasn't a miracle," I said.

"Anyway, quick recovery. You probably shouldn't be downstairs. And do me a favor. If you can help it, please don't breathe on the kids. You guys should stay apart for a few days so as not to pass this illness back and forth. Miles and Flora can read and hang out. Jack, you should go back to bed."

Just the sight of them made me mad, the three of them having their perfect, healthy gourmet breakfast with their perfect cook in their perfect kitchen. Even if they'd had a bad experience with their previous household staff, even if Miles acted out in some way and got kicked out of school, it was better than what Lucy went through. Poor Lucy had wound up dead. And all because of Norris.

I almost wished Norris was still alive so I could kill him all over again. Meanwhile, in whatever other realm she inhabited, maybe suspended in some zone between the worlds of the dead and the living, Lucy needed my protection. That's why she visited me last night. If only I'd known her when she was alive, maybe none of this would have happened.

Linda said, "Jack, you need to rest. You should spend the day in bed. I'll bring you a tray upstairs—"

I said, "You're not my mother." I ran outside, slamming the screen door behind me.

"I can lend you a book," Miles called after me. "A cool book about explorers."

"Keep it," I yelled back. "You think I care about your stupid, boring explorers?"

I waited on the doorstep, not knowing where to go next. I heard Linda say, "Jeez, what did I do? What's got into him?"

"It's nothing *you* did," said Miles.

"He's probably still feeling sick," said Flora.

That was it. That was too much. I ran off across

the back lawn.

I felt a little better outside, away from them and breathing the fresh air. I went and sat by the lake. I focused on the spot near the boathouse where Lucy appeared when I was with Flora. I hoped she'd come back, now that I was alone. I kept staring at that same place. I didn't want to miss her.

Sometime in the afternoon—I'd left my watch inside—Flora appeared and asked if I wanted lunch.

"Leave me alone!" I said. "Can't any of you leave me be?" Normally, I would have felt bad for shouting at Flora. But if anything had been normal, I wouldn't have shouted at Flora.

"We're worried about you," she said. "Linda told me to come check on you."

"Worry about yourself," I said. "I'll see you when I see you."

I spent the rest of the afternoon sitting by the lake, under a tree. Finally I gave up. Lucy wasn't going to appear. Norris had probably found out about last night, and somewhere—wherever they were—he was holding her prisoner.

When I got back to the house, the three of them were in the kitchen. Had they been there all day, talking about me? Why couldn't they back off and give me a little breathing room, so I could get my head together?

On the table in a jar was one of Flora's disgusting wildflower bouquets. Considering that they always wilted the minute she brought them into the house, this one looked relatively fresh. So I figured she must have found something to do without me following her around as she ran from flower to flower showing off how much she knew about what the nasty weeds were called in Latin. As if anyone cared, as if anyone spoke Latin anymore, as if anyone would know if she was making it all up!

Miles had brought his book to the table, so I assumed he'd been reading about explorers, which struck me as a pathetic activity for a kid who never got to go anywhere by himself, who wasn't allowed to leave the island, and who'd gotten expelled from school and sent back the first time he'd escaped. And Linda was making her oh-so-special pasta, when the truth is, I prefer my dad's spaghetti, even the ravioli he heats up from a can when he's been working too hard to cook.

Linda glanced up when I walked in. She said, "Jack, you look awful! You look like you've seen a ghost!" As soon as she said it, she realized what she'd said. "Oh, I'm so sorry. It's just that you're so pale, and you've been outdoors all day, so—"

"I was in the shade," I said. "Trying to breathe." I guess I shouldn't have said that, because as soon as I did, my chest began to hurt, and I heard myself gasp, as if I couldn't breathe.

"Listen to you!" said Linda. "My God! I think the flu's gone down into your chest. If it doesn't clear up by the weekend, I'm taking you to a doctor."

"Don't threaten me," I said.

"Jack! Stop it. You're scaring the children! Go to bed right now!" Linda said sharply.

I was going to tell her to get lost, but I caught a look in her eye. . . . She looked pretty scared herself. I decided I'd better shut up and leave.

"Get some rest, Jack," Miles called after me.

And Flora said, "Yes, get some sleep."

I almost asked, Are you real kids? What kind of children sound like that, talking in superpolite grown-up voices? But I didn't say that, or anything. And later I was glad.

I was feeling a little guilty as I went up to my room. Linda and Miles and Flora had never been anything but kind to me. It wasn't their fault I'd spent the day wanting to see a person who doesn't exist. It was crazy, how much I wanted to see her.

I'm glad I can say this, Sophie. It's a good thing we've broken up, because otherwise there would be so much I had to hide. I know that you and I were happy together, and we had some nice times. But I have to tell you that what I felt about you was nothing compared to what I feel about Lucy. That desperate wanting to see the person . . . I hope you don't think I'm being heartless. Because I don't want to be cruel to you or Linda or Miles or Flora. I'm a good person, you know that. I don't understand what's going on. It's like I'm under a spell here.

Or maybe it's like Linda says: maybe I'm still sick.

In fact that night I was really sick. I could tell that my fever was coming back. And strangely enough, I was happy. Every chill and ache and burning pain made me think that Lucy was connected with it, and maybe I would get to see her again.

I think I'd better stop now. But I want to tell you one thing: If you tell my dad one word of this, you're going to be sorry.

Jack

DEAR JACK,

You're really scaring me now. Maybe this is all a joke, but it doesn't sound like one. Look, we can break up if you want to. I'll be sad about it, but I'll understand. And it's not true that I'm seeing Josh again. I don't know how to make you believe me. But if you don't want to be with me . . . okay. People grow apart. But, Jack, please read over your last letter. Look at what you said.

You're breaking up with me because you've fallen in love with a woman who was murdered? None of it sounds like you—all that anger and resentment toward Linda and the kids. Maybe it is some physical illness, like Linda says. Or maybe the strain was more than you knew, entertaining the kids and being so isolated and our being apart. Maybe something snapped in you. It happens. I never imagined it happening to someone like you, but I guess I didn't know you that well. I can see that now.

Maybe some kind of time bomb went off inside your brain. Isn't that what happened to your mother? Maybe it has something to do with your mom dying when you were so young, and now you're obsessed with a dead woman.

But like I said, you're scaring me. I want you to write me right now and tell me you're feeling better and sound like a sane person again. It's still all right if you want to break up. I can deal with it. But I can't stand being this worried.

I promise not to tell your dad. At least not for a while. I know you didn't mean it when you said you were going to make me sorry. I want you to feel that there's someone you can talk to. Even if I'm not physically there. But if I don't hear from you pretty soon, and if you don't sound better, or if you don't tell Linda about all this crazy stuff you're imagining, I'm going to have to tell someone. Someone's going to have to help you.

Write to me soon.

Love,

Sophie

DEAR SOPHIE,

Well, I guess I finally know what it takes to get your attention. I have to fall in love with someone else. And maybe you wouldn't even care if I'd hooked up with another girl. The fact that it's a dead woman—well, that got you writing.

I'm glad you wrote, but you know what? You can forget the Freudian crap about my mom dying being the reason why this is happening. Just like you can save the unbelievably tasteless joke about the bomb exploding in my mother's head. And you and Josh can get back together and get married someday for all I care. But you're right about it being a bad idea for me to be mad at Linda and the kids. I'll try to keep that under control. I don't know why I'm even writing to you, Sophie. Maybe it's just like a bad habit I can't break.

Where was I? Oh, right. The night I got sick again or had that relapse or whatever.

I made myself stay awake, thinking it was the fever that had brought Lucy last time, so maybe it would work again. But the fever was stronger than I was. My eyes hurt. I was blinking. . . .

Someone was there, sitting on the bed.

"You came back," I said.

"I had to," Lucy said. "I want to give you something. And I want to say more about . . . what happened with the kids. About that card game where our hearts got ripped apart every time we lost."

"What about it?"

"Norris used to try and turn Miles and Flora against each other. Every so often he'd make them say terrible things about each other, horrifying reasons why they hated each other."

I said, "They seem okay with it now."

"They aren't," she said. "Believe me, they aren't okay."

"Miles got kicked out of school," I said.

"We know that."

"What do you mean 'we'? Where's Norris? Where is he now?"

I couldn't see very well in the dark, but I could hear Lucy sniffling. "He's still in the bar."

"What bar?"

"Where it happened." Lucy was crying now. "The shooting. I know Linda told you about that. Have you been to Norris's cottage?"

"No," I said. "I never wanted to. There was never any reason to go there."

"You should. There's something you could learn there."

I said, "I'll go tomorrow." I tried to keep my voice steady, not just because I felt sick. But because, after everything that had happened, I was scared to go to the cottage, and I didn't want Lucy to know. "Is that where it is?"

"Where what is?" I heard her breathing in the dark. It seemed odd that ghosts needed to breathe.

"The thing you came to give me."

"No. I have that here with me."

"What is it?"

"A medal," said Lucy. "A holy medal."

"What kind?" I don't know much about holy medals. Dad's some kind of Protestant, but he stopped going to church after Mom died. He hardly ever went before, except sometimes when Mom did. Which wasn't very often.

"It's a St. Jude medal," Lucy said. "The patron saint of lost causes and hopeless cases."

"Thanks a lot," I said. "Is that what you think of me? A hopeless case?" I waited for Lucy to laugh, just to be polite. I don't know why I expected a ghost to have a sense of humor or to care about politeness.

"I was the hopeless case," Lucy said. "And I thought Norris was my hope. But after I let him into my life, I was more hopeless than ever."

It was the saddest thing I ever heard. I wanted to

say, I can make you happy. But what would I have said next? And how could I make a dead person happy? I guess I wasn't thinking very clearly.

"I've had this medal since I was a little girl. And it brought me luck—what little luck I had. It rescued me, sort of. I liked my life here, I liked the kids, I liked Linda. It was better than my life before. I don't want to talk about my old life. I wouldn't have got the job here unless I lied to Jim Crackstone. And he didn't check out my references. He didn't want to be bothered. But Norris was my bad luck. When I left the island to follow him, I almost gave the medal to Flora. But I was scared to give it away. I took it with me. And for a while my luck held. I got a job teaching school on the mainland—"

"Linda told me that, too," I said. It was all coming back to me now. I knew where this was going.

"I guess my luck might have kept improving, if I'd been smart. If I'd left Norris. Things with Norris were deteriorating daily. It didn't help that he was gambling more and more. And he'd started losing big-time. The guys he was playing against were in a whole different league from me and Miles and Flora. And the stakes they played for weren't soul-destroying secrets but serious money. Which mattered more to these guys than secrets. And they weren't scared of Norris, like we were.

"One night Norris was losing badly. Everyone was drinking, which these guys usually didn't do when they were playing. But they must have figured that Norris was on such a losing streak, they could have played with half their brains pickled in alcohol, and they'd still take all his money.

"I was there at the table with them. He liked me to be with him, and I went, though I knew that pretty soon my presence at those games was going to cost me my teaching job. But I didn't care about anything but Norris. I know how insane that was."

I said, "I know what that's like, Lucy." And then I got really embarrassed because what I meant is that I felt that way about Lucy. I would have done anything, anything she asked.

She said, "I'd sort of stopped paying attention when I heard Norris say, 'I guess it's hopeless.'

Norris fell silent. Then he said, 'Why didn't I think of that before?' The saint of hopeless cases. Lucy! Let's bet your medal.'

"He told the other players, 'Gentleman, I have one more thing to bet against . . . to bet against whatever you think will match it. My lady friend's lifesaving medal. It works miracles for its lucky owner. Like my girlfriend here. The one who's always crying.'"

"Where is he?" I asked Lucy. "Tell me. I'll go punch him out, I swear."

Lucy didn't seem to hear, or maybe she just ignored me.

She said, "I told Norris no. I wouldn't let him bet my medal. It was the first time I'd ever refused him anything. And the sound of my own voice saying no finally woke me up. The medal was in my pocket. I grabbed it and held on to it. I told Norris I was leaving. I needed to step outside and get some air. He said, 'That's what you think.' He came after me. We started arguing and fighting. I knew he wouldn't hurt me, not with those other guys watching.

"Everyone started shouting, saying that Norris and I weren't really fighting. They said we were just pretending. Someone yelled that this was all a trick, an act we'd cooked up to distract them from the game and wreck their concentration. Now that they were distracted, Norris was going to win.

"I heard someone say, 'Put that gun away.' There was more shouting, and then it happened. It hurt for a second. I felt like something was leaving my body, rushing out of me. Then, just like that, it was over. There was no more pain. I was floating above myself, looking down at myself. . . ."

"I'm sorry, Lucy" was all I could say.

"Don't be," she said. "It's not so awful. It's really not. You get used to it pretty quickly."

"Being dead?" I asked. But she didn't answer.

"Maybe it's a bad luck medal," I said. "That's what it sounds like to me."

"Trust me, Jack," she said. "I know these things. And I want you to have it."

It killed me when she said my name. I was so

choked up I could hardly speak. I held out my hand in the dark.

"I'm sorry," she said. "I can't touch you. It's against the rules."

"You can't touch me?" I said. "Not even to give me something?"

"I can't," she said. "It's the first rule. I can't even risk it. I'll leave the medal on your night table."

"Thank you," I said.

I blinked. I opened my eyes. The morning sun was blazing in my window. I heard the seagulls cry.

Ha-ha. Fooled you.

Jack

DEAR JACK,

Your last letter scared me even worse than the letter before. I think I should tell your dad. I think you need help. I want your permission to tell him. I still care about you.

Love,

Sophie

DEAR SOPHIE,

Permission to do what? Permission to get me declared legally out of my mind? Is that what you think? That I've gone off the deep end? Do you think I don't realize that this is something you do? Something you like to do? You go out with guys and then dump them and drive them crazy. Don't you think I know that Josh spent time in rehab after you broke up? Which he's out of now, so you two can get back together, and you can do the same thing to him all over again. Well, you're not going to do it to me!!! You don't have my permission!!!

Anyway, you'd have trouble convincing someone I'm crazy when now I have physical evidence that what's happened to me is real. That evidence is beside my laptop on the desk as I write this.

When I woke up in the morning, I was afraid to look. So I reached out my hand. I felt it.

Lucy's holy medal.

It's tiny. An oval silver frame around a full color image of the saint. To be honest, St. Jude doesn't look all that special. If I was sitting next to the guy on a train or in a waiting room, I don't know if I'd be interested enough to start a conversation. But that's not the point. The point is that it was Lucy's, and she loved it more than anything. And she gave it to me. She gave me more than you ever did!

I brought it over to the window. There was a little red streak on the glass over the picture of the saint. I knew it was Lucy's blood.

Maybe it did work miracles. Because I felt totally cured. I got dressed and went downstairs.

Linda said, "You look a million times better!"

"I feel a million times better," I said. "It's like a miracle cure."

Linda gave me a searching look. I remembered she'd said that yesterday, about the miracle cure. Did she think I was making fun of her? But it did feel like a miracle. Thank you, saint of hopeless cases.

"I'm joking," I said. "Where are the kids?"

"Still sleeping, I think," said Linda. "You're up early. Didn't you notice how early it is?"

"Actually, no," I said. "But listen, I want to apologize. For being crabby. It's just that I was feeling so sick. I'm sure I said hurtful things to you and the kids that I didn't mean at all."

"That's okay," said Linda. "Everyone gets cranky when they're sick. There were days when my husband . . . well, let's not think about that. Let's just remember the good times. Anyhow, why not take another day off to recuperate? The kids can take it easy, too, and you can relax and rest and finish recovering before you go back to hanging out with them tomorrow."

"That sounds great," I said. "I've been wanting to take a walk. To go into the woods and think and be quiet."

Was Linda staring at me again? I couldn't look her in the eye.

"Are you hungry?" she asked me.

"I could eat something," I said.

In fact I wasn't hungry. But I faked it, scarfing down two slices of toast and a plate of eggs. It was all I could do not to gag. It wasn't that I still felt sick, but I was nervous about going to Norris's cottage.

I would learn something there, Lucy had said. She hadn't said something good. But I didn't care how bad it might be. I wanted to know what it was.

I waited a suitable amount of time so that Linda would think I was digesting my food instead of rushing outside to carry out an assignment I'd gotten from a ghost.

"I guess I'll be heading out," I said.

"Will you be back for lunch?" asked Linda.

"I'll only be gone a little while," I said. "I don't want to push it." I reached into my pocket and touched the St. Jude medal for good luck.

"That sounds sensible," Linda told me. "See you in a while. It's good you have nice weather."

I wanted to say, Listen, if I don't come back by noon, please send someone to find me. But that would probably alarm Linda so much she'd make me go back to bed and stay there. Anyway, who was she going to send to find me, and what was going to happen to me on an island where there were no other people? Was I scared of getting lost?

You'd have to be pretty messed up to get lost. Even the marshes were covered by the zigzag path.

In case Linda was watching, I tried to give the impression of being a regular person taking a leisurely walk with no particular destination in mind. I knew that by the time I got to the lakeshore she couldn't see me anymore. Even so, I sat down in the shade of the tree so Linda would think I was taking it easy and resting.

But of course the reason I stopped there had nothing to do with Linda. I was still hoping that Lucy would appear on the bank, near the boathouse. We could spend the day talking, and I could forget about going to Norris's cottage. Maybe I could persuade Lucy to break that rule against touching. Laws were made to be broken. There were probably laws against coming back to the world of the living and messing with the heads of guys like me. I would talk her out of the not-touching rule, and we could lie there and whisper and kiss all day. Like we used to do, Sophie, remember?

Should I not be telling you this, Sophie? Is it

harsh of me to say all this? Well, it's okay, I know you don't care anymore, anyway. And in return for reading this and for letting me be so honest, you can tell me what you're doing with Josh. Deal?

Once more I stared at the spot where Lucy had been. Only today I looked harder, willing her to appear. It was like a meditation, and sure enough, my mind emptied out except for one annoying thought. What if Linda was just saying I should take another day off? What if I'd gotten so obviously weird that Linda was nervous about my being alone with the kids? And she'd sent me out for a walk so she could figure out the next step. What if she was about to break the don't-bother–Jim Crackstone law or deal with the problem herself, like she'd done with Norris? What if she was planning to make my dad come and get me, so I could go home in disgrace, with the whole town—including you, Sophie—knowing how badly I'd screwed up? Though I guess you already think that. Maybe you're the crazy one, after all.

But I promise. No, I swear: There's no reason to

worry. There's no problem at all about my being alone with Miles and Flora.

I decided to move on. Lucy wasn't coming back. I didn't blame her. Why should she come visit me when I couldn't concentrate on her without worrying about what Linda was thinking about me and the children? I didn't deserve to see Lucy, and besides, she belonged to Norris.

Maybe the thing I would learn in the cottage was the secret that would save her. Maybe she was sending me on a mission that would break the hold that Norris had over her, even in the other world.

I knew how to get to Norris's cottage. I just didn't want to go. But I knew why I had to go, and it gave me the courage I needed.

I felt as if Lucy was guiding me. I touched her medal for courage.

I could tell that no one had been on the path for a while. That is, no living person. And if a ghost had come this way, it hadn't bothered clearing away the roots and branches. Once I slipped on a patch of slick mud, and once I tripped over a place where brambles had grown across the path.

The weathered cottage was covered with thorny briars and dead ivy. Weeds had grown up all around it. The cottage hadn't been cared for, or cared about, in a long time.

To tell the truth, I was more worried about animals than about spirits or ghosts. It was just the sort of place where raccoons or bats or squirrels would nest. Even if they had moved on, there would be gnawed-up bones and animal shit. It looked like somewhere rats would go to die.

I pulled some branches away from the entrance and took a deep breath and pushed. The door was swollen shut. I had to lean all my weight against it, until finally the door opened—and I fell inside.

Nothing scurried or fluttered. There were no raccoons. No nesting birds. And as far as I could tell, no dead rats.

The place smelled like a cave—mushroomy, dank, and wet. Someone had left in a hurry. It was impossible to tell the garbage from the possessions Norris had discarded: broken dishes and beer bottles, scraps of paper and old clothes with a strange flower design that turned out to be patches of mildew. The cottage was like a crime scene, only without any corpses or blood. The ripped-up dirty magazines gave me the creeps. I noticed the pool cues leaning against the wall. So this was where all the pool cues had gone! Why had Norris needed pool cues out here in the cottage, where there wasn't even a pool table? I didn't want to know.

At first I couldn't believe that neat, perfect, well-behaved Miles and Flora would want to hang out here. But the more I thought about it, the easier it was to understand. What a relief it must have been to be surrounded by all this mess after spending their lives dressed like old-fashioned dolls, under the constant pressure of Linda's suffocatingly warm, superorderly, motherly niceness.

But even if Miles and Flora liked it here, it definitely made me jumpy. I kept looking back over my shoulder. What if Norris knew I was here, in his former home? If Lucy could come back, so could he. And I'd seen him—twice. What if he followed me and found me and there was no one around and—?

Just then the door banged shut.

"Please," I heard myself saying. "Please." But who was I talking to, and what was I asking? Obviously, I was losing it. It was only the wind that had slammed the door. I was alone in the cottage. Safe, at least for the moment. But I was sure that if I stayed any longer, something awful would happen. I had to get out fast.

I started talking to Lucy, even though she wasn't there. I said, "What did you mean? What can I learn in this horrible place? Why did you tell me to come here?"

Something powerful whipped me around, like my own private indoor tornado.

"Lucy, is that you? What do you want me to do?" I could tell where the force—or whatever it was—wanted me to look. In the filthy kitchen was a refrigerator. The door had been torn off, and I could see furry scraps of what had once been food (I hoped it was former food) on the moldy shelves. On the wall beside the refrigerator was a hook. And on the hook was a key.

I said, "Is that it?" I took Lucy's medal out of my pocket and closed my eyes and squeezed the image of the saint as hard as I could.

I swear to you, Sophie. I heard Lucy's voice.

"The schoolroom," Lucy said.

I put the key in my pocket.

I know what you're thinking, Sophie. Jack's seeing things; he's hearing things. He's totally lost his mind. But you know what? I've never felt so sane. So calm and reasonable and logical. And you know what proves it, Sophie? When I heard Lucy mention the schoolroom, I didn't even have to stop and wonder where the schoolroom was, or why Flora and Miles or Linda had never mentioned that there was a schoolroom. It took me about two seconds to understand that it was just another one of the secrets they'd conspired to keep from me. But I'm smarter than they are, and with Lucy's help, everything was finally becoming obvious. Very obvious. Painfully clear, you could say.

I headed back toward the house. I didn't exactly feel like myself. I felt more . . . well, kind of like a wolf. Watchful, quick, alert.

From a distance, I saw that Linda and Miles and Flora were all working in the garden. I watched them for a few minutes, and I thought, Man, those golf clubs are really ugly! She's made that beautiful garden look like a dead golf-club graveyard.

The fact that all three of them were out there together was pretty unusual. Normally, Linda did all the planting and weeding and picking by herself. I guess Miles and Flora didn't like to get their little hands dirty.

Once again, I had the feeling that it had something to do with me. That Linda had decided to keep the kids close to her in case I came back to the house. It was just more evidence that she'd started thinking I was out of control and a danger to the children. Which I am totally not!!! Although it's funny, Sophie. People should be careful what they think you are, because the more they think you're something bad, the greater the chances of you becoming that bad thing. Know what I mean?

Anyhow, I was glad they were all outside and wouldn't get in my way or annoy me or offer me some delicious food I didn't want to eat. I certainly didn't want the kids asking to go with me when I'd finally figured out how to get inside the schoolroom.

Even though no one was inside the house, I was very quiet going up the stairs. I didn't want Norris's ghost to know where I was headed. My only hope was that Lucy was somehow distracting him, or that—wherever he was—he'd reached the point of no longer caring what happened on the island. But if that was true, why had he come back, looking—I was sure now—for Miles? I decided not to think about that and just to keep my mind on what I had to do.

I knew where the schoolroom was. It had to be the locked room. The door the kids had tried to open my first afternoon on the island. The only room that they—by "they" I guess I mean Linda— still kept locked.

The key fit perfectly. I started to turn it, then stopped. Started again, then stopped. I felt as if everything that had happened to me on the island had been leading to this moment, that every mystery and unanswered question would be resolved when I unlocked that door.

So you can imagine how disappointed I was when it turned out to look like . . . well, like a schoolroom. Though to tell you the truth, Sophie, and now that we've broken up, I feel like I can tell you the truth and not have to act like the big, strong guy, the brave, fearless boyfriend . . . I almost wrote *boy fiend*. A little misspelling, I guess. So maybe it was a good thing I was in a schoolroom, where someone like myself could learn the difference between *boyfriend* and *boy fiend*.

Now where was I? Right. I was relieved. I wasn't ready to deal with another crime scene like Norris's cottage. And the schoolroom was pretty ordinary, pretty neat: A blackboard. Two little school desks with attached seats—remember we had those desks in first grade, before they renovated the school?

Did we even know each other in first grade? I suddenly can't remember. The room smelled of chalk dust and little kids. Maybe I was imagining it, but underneath, there was a faint scent of that hand cream Lucy used. All in all, kind of pleasant. So what did Lucy want me to find?

The more I looked around, the more everything seemed just a little . . . off. Maybe it would have seemed normal if I didn't know Miles and Flora. On one wall was a huge map. Not a map of the world or of the United States, but a map of Outer Mongolia. There were botanical charts everywhere, pictures of flowers and plants with their Latin names. They were old, extremely old. They looked as if they'd been torn out of the kind of books that contain spells and recipes for magic potions that wizards could concoct from . . . flowers and plants. There were images of volcanoes that must have been there from the time of Jim Crackstone, posters of animals and birds. . . .

And here's where things started to get weird. On one wall was a blown-up photograph of a seagull. I swear to you, it was the same bird that had yelled at me on the boat.

My legs started feeling funny, and I sat down at one of the little desks. It was the kind with the top that flips open. Inside was a crumpled sheet of notebook paper. I closed the lid again and smoothed the paper out on the desktop.

Up in one corner, it said *Flora Crackstone. Miss Lucy Jessel's class. Winter essay.*

So that was her name. Jessel. Only now I realized that I'd never known her last name. Linda had never even bothered with it. To Linda she was just Lucy. Poor dead Lucy.

Flora's handwriting was exactly what I would have expected. Neat printing, precise, perfect, no nonsense, no circles over the *i*'s. The title of her composition was "The History of Crackstone's Landing."

Many amazing people have lived on our island, from heroes of the American Revolution to Robert Crackstone, one of the earliest archaeologists to visit Pompeii and dig up all the dead Roman people who'd been buried by the volcano.

But it's also true that a couple of bad things have happened on our island. People talk about the Crackstone curse, but in my opinion there's no such thing. Everything that happened here was not because of supernatural powers but because of some bad thing that someone did.

In 1929, Louisa Crackstone, the youngest daughter of James Crackstone III, fell in love with the gardener, a man by the name of Nolan. From the first time she met him, she felt he had a magical power over her. And she was lost. There was nothing she could do. Theirs was a true love, a real love. But the family disapproved. The couple tried to elope by boat, but a big wave came up and drowned them.

The family was really sorry. They should have let them get married.

That was where Flora's essay stopped. On the bottom, in red pencil, it said, *A+. Excellent job.*

Lucy had touched the page I was holding in my hands. She had held it and written on it.

It's funny, Sophie. Even though we're broken up, it's like I still have your voice in my head, like when we were together. So I can hear your thoughts collecting around some kind of outrage about Lucy teaching innocent little Flora a story about a woman who falls under some guy's power and dies because of it. I can hear you thinking, What kind of story is that for a little girl to hear—and write? But you know what, Sophie? I'm sick of your girl-power crap. What was Flora supposed to write? A composition about the first woman president of the United States? Well, guess what, there was no woman president of the United States. And I think the story that Lucy probably told her and that she wrote was a very beautiful story. And you've got to admit that the way it was written is impressive for a girl Flora's age.

I put Flora's paper back in the desk, quickly, almost as if I was scared she was going to catch me reading it. Trying to calm down, I told myself that the picture on the wall couldn't have been the same seagull that I saw on the boat. All seagulls look pretty much alike. It was just a coincidence that there was a picture of one on the wall. Not even a coincidence. The island was in the middle of the ocean. There were seagulls everywhere. Duh.

But I guess I was still on edge. Anyone who saw me from the outside—and I was so afraid that Norris's ghost might be watching from the windows that I couldn't look at the windows—might have thought I was really nervous. I roamed around the room, looking at everything, picking up everything. Every pencil, every piece of chalk, every eraser and empty notebook was a whole education for me. I could imagine myself back in this classroom, when everything was still innocent. When Flora was writing her composition, and Lucy was giving her an A+, and Miles was staring up at the map of Outer Mongolia and thinking about some story Norris had told him.

Some story Norris had told him. It was never innocent.

Norris had been making Lucy very unhappy, forcing her to play that cruel card game. And making the children play, too.

Or maybe I was just thinking this because I was looking at the cards.

I had wandered over to a little table, a square table with four chairs, the kind of table at which kids finger paint and make their lumpy art projects from clay and Play-Doh. The cards were dealt out in hands, seven cards at each of four places. The rest of the deck was in the middle of table.

They weren't regular cards. They were death cards. The suits were the regular four suits—hearts, diamonds, spades, and clubs. But there were skeletons holding the hearts. The clubs were grinning skulls. The diamonds were gravestones. And the spades were tiny images of shovels digging graves.

Beside the cards were piles of pebbles like the ones I'd seen at the lakeshore. And it gave me the chills, because I remembered learning in school how in some places they leave stones by the graves of their loved ones, sort of like messages saying that the living relatives had been there to visit.

I picked the cards up; I put them down; I was careful not to disturb them, as if the game was still in progress and someone might get angry if I messed up his hand.

Or maybe I just thought that because I saw something that I should have noticed before. In the middle of the card table was a glass jelly jar, and in the jelly jar was a bouquet of wildflowers. They were fresh, or as near to fresh as Flora's bouquets ever were.

The children had been here recently. Were they still playing that hideous card game? Were they playing it with the ghosts of Norris and Lucy? If the ghosts could appear to me, why couldn't they make themselves known to the children? Had the children been pretending when they'd acted as if they hadn't seen Lucy on the shore or Norris in the tower? I looked at the cards and the wildflower bouquet.

Suddenly, I knew. I knew what had happened. I knew what was still happening.

Everything was clear.

I grabbed a fistful of cards and shoved them in my pocket. Then I went out to the garden. Lucy and Flora and Miles were still there, weeding and digging. They were happy and smiling, but I knew that they would stop smiling once they heard what I had to tell them.

I let the garden gate close behind me. Did I imagine they shrank back when they saw me? Well, of course they were startled: I'd crept up on them from nowhere. And I can hardly imagine how filthy and freaked out I looked after a morning in Norris's cottage and then my discovery in the schoolroom.

I said, "I know what happened. You can't fool me anymore. It's a creepy feeling to be lied to by little children. And maybe it only worked because all three of you were in on it. Conspiring. But it's over. I know now, I know everything—"

"Jack, what do you know?" said Linda. The kids were hiding behind her, peeking out at me. Like terrified babies. "What's over? You poor thing, you look so drawn and pale. I don't think you're getting better. . . . I think we need to get you to a doctor."

"Sure," I said. "Take me to a doctor who's working for Jim Crackstone, some quack who'll say I'm out of my mind and hallucinating all this. But I'm not imagining things. I understand it better than you do, Linda. Or maybe better than you're pretending."

"Please, Jack, don't yell at Linda," Flora said.

"Miles!" I said. "Stop hiding behind Linda for a change."

Obedient as ever, Miles stepped out from behind his fake mommy.

I said, "I know what happened in your school. I know why they don't want you back there."

"They don't want me back? Linda, what does he mean?"

I don't know why it hadn't occurred to me that Linda still hadn't told him. When was she going to announce it? The night before he was supposed to leave for school in the fall, when he was all packed and ready to go?

"Jack," said Linda. "I can't believe you're doing

this. What's gotten into you? What's wrong?"

"Don't make me laugh," I said. "It's the card game, isn't it, Miles? You taught the other kids at school to play that evil game. And the school found out about it, right? What happened? Did you destroy one of the other boys the way Norris destroyed Lucy? Did you play for their souls? And when you won their souls, Miles, what did you do with them?"

"Souls?" said Miles. "We played for pennies."

"You played card games at school? What did you play, Miles?" said Linda.

"Poker," said Miles. "Norris taught us. We'd play for pebbles at his cottage. Pebbles from the lakeshore. He told us that out in the real world people played for real money. So when I got to school I taught some of the other boys, though a lot of them knew already. I'm sorry I used some of Uncle Jim's allowance, but I never won or lost more than a dollar the whole time I was there. But one kid lost a quarter in one night, and he got mad, though not because of the money. I guess he just didn't like

losing. So he told the principal, who called everyone into his office, one by one. And someone—I
don't know who—told on me. I said I was sorry. I
thought the whole thing was over. I can't believe
they wrote to you and told you they didn't want me
to come back. It was just a few pennies!"

"Is that all?" Linda said. "Your school made it
sound a whole lot worse than that." Linda couldn't
help looking at me, because she and I were the only
ones who knew the school had used the word *evil*.

"I swear to you," Miles said. "On my life and
Flora's and yours and—" Little baby Miles had
started crying. Linda bent down and hugged him.
What a touching sight! I thought I was going to be
sick.

"I think your school overreacted," she said. "I
knew it was some kind of church school. Very
strict. Otherwise your uncle Jim wouldn't have sent
you there. So maybe they have very high standards.
Maybe something like that seemed worse to them
than it might have at another place. But you know
it wasn't good. Kids shouldn't gamble, Miles. It was

wrong of you to teach them. . . ."

"I'm sorry," said Miles. "I told them I was sorry."

"Are you sorry for lying?" I said. "Because that's what you're doing right now. And if I were you, I'd be a little worried about having sworn on everyone's life. If anything that I've been saying is true, you're all going to wind up dead."

Miles hid behind Linda again. "Jack, stop it!" Linda said. "What's wrong with you? Go back into the house."

I ignored her. I said, "You know that's all a big lie about playing for pennies. You know what you were playing for, just like you know that you and Flora are still playing that evil card game. You're still playing it in the schoolroom with Norris and Lucy. I saw Flora's bouquet there."

Flora cried out from behind Linda, "Please, Jack, stop. You're frightening us. We haven't been in the schoolroom since Kate left."

"Let me get this straight," I said. "I'm scary, but playing cards with two dead people isn't scary? You think those cards aren't scary? You think I don't know they're special cards? You think I don't know what they look like?"

"Jack! What are you talking about? What cards?" asked Linda.

"If you don't believe me, look!" I said. I grabbed the cards from my pocket and threw them on the ground. The skulls looked up at me, and the skeletons with their bleeding hearts, and the gravestones and the shovels. "You call those ordinary cards, Miles? They're death cards!"

"But, Jack," said Linda. "They are ordinary cards. Diamonds, hearts, spades, clubs. A regular pack of playing cards."

So now I was completely surrounded by people trying to make me think I'd gone insane. I wanted to ask Linda why she was lying. I wanted to ask the kids if they thought they were regular playing cards, too. But I knew the children would lie, just like they always had. I wanted to make them admit that they were seeing Lucy and Norris and to ask Flora how her little bouquet got into the locked schoolroom when—

That was when I saw him. Norris had come for the children or for Lucy or to take revenge on all of us on the island. Maybe the cards had called him. I had no idea how he'd gotten there. But somehow I knew he meant to harm us.

Norris was walking across the lawn, looking straight at me. He was taller and stronger than I remembered from the boat and way more frightening than he'd seemed in the window and on the tower. He was obviously furious. I asked myself whether I was brave and strong enough to fight Norris—to fight a ghost. He seemed to get bigger as he approached. I didn't think I could win.

Finally, he was so close that I could see his eyes, and I knew: they were the cold, black, beady eyes of the seagull that had warned me not to go to the island.

I wondered what he'd done with Lucy. Had she tried to stop him from coming after us? Were they in different places? Did she know? Or had he managed to hurt her even in another world, even after death?

"Get out of here!" I yelled.

"Jack! Who are yelling at?" said Linda.

"Don't pretend you don't see him," I said. "Don't any of you pretend. But I'll protect you, don't worry. That's why I was hired. That's why Jim Crackstone brought me here. He knew that this would happen. And he knew that I was the only one who could see it happening and prevent it."

I don't know if I even believed this. I don't know what I believed. I was talking to calm myself down. Norris was coming closer.

He slammed into the garden.

"Get back," I told the kids.

"You can't hide from me," Norris said. His voice was low. He reached toward me, lunged at me. Could a ghost actually touch me? Hurt me? Was he planning to take me with him to the other world? Me and Linda and the children? Would Hank the gardener find our bodies when he and his men came to work? Jim Crackstone would have to tell my dad that I was dead because he insisted on keeping two children prisoners on a cursed island where tragedies kept on happening.

I grabbed for something, anything. I felt one of Linda's husband's golf clubs sticking out of the ground. I yanked it free and raised it above my head.

"Get the hell out," I told Norris.

Norris disappeared. But he was a ghost. He could do that. He appeared again, on the other side of the kids. Linda and the children stood between me and Norris.

"Get out of the way," I told them. I let Norris see that I had the golf club and that I meant to use it. It crossed my mind that he wouldn't care. He was dead already. Then I let the thought go. There was nothing else I could do.

I advanced toward Norris. He watched me approach and started to laugh.

"You think this is funny?" I said.

Then everything got very warm.

The sun blinked out. The world went dark.

EDGEWATER

DEAR DAD,

The rule was I had to wait two weeks before I could write you. Maybe it's just to see if the crazies here (like me!!) know what day it is, so we can tell when two weeks have passed. Which would mean we're sane enough to start reestablishing contact with the outside world.

I wish I could have written to you before. There's been so much I've wanted to say. But maybe it's good for me to have had this time to sort out what happened to me on the island.

Dad, it was really strange to wake up in my bed in my room on the island and see you leaning over me, frowning and worried, saying, "Jack, Jack, please wake up."

"I'm awake," I said. "My head hurts. What happened? What are you doing here, Dad?"

You said, "It's not clear, Jack. We're still trying to

figure it out. It seems you had some kind of episode. Jim Crackstone sent a doctor out on the ferry with me. According to the doctor, you had a little . . . break with reality. And we need to figure out what caused it. If it's something physical or mental or—"

I touched the sore spot on the back of my head. It's a shock to discover a painful Ping-Pong ball bulging straight out of your skull.

"What's this?" I asked. "This bump back here?"

Linda and the kids said that I was yelling and threatening them with a golf club. Linda knew she had to defend the children. She yanked another club out of the ground and hit me from behind, not hard enough to seriously injure me but hard enough to knock me out cold.

I said, "I wasn't threatening the kids. I was defending them from Norris."

You asked me who Norris was, and I told you he was a guy who used to work on the island. You asked me if he'd come back to the island recently, or since I got there, or what.

"Dad," I said. "Don't you get it? The guy is

dead. It was his ghost."

"That's our problem right there," you said.

You know the next part, Dad. Jim Crackstone's doctor came in to talk to me, and he asked if I wanted something to make me feel better. I knew it was a bad idea. I knew it meant they were going to drug me. They'd probably take me off the island and lock me up somewhere. But you know what? By then I would have gone for anything that anyone promised would make me feel better.

I dimly remember the ferry ride. You stayed with me for the whole trip. You kept saying I'd be fine. I remember checking into this hospital or treatment center or whatever this is. I remember someone in a white coat saying that I'd had a serious infection and also that I hadn't slept for a long time. Which was strange. Because I was pretty sure I had slept. I remember sleeping on the island with the sounds of the waves in my ears and waking up to the cries of the seagulls. But already I was figuring out that I was probably the last person who knew what had really happened—to me!

A few days after I got here, I started seeing Dr. Lee, who's quiet and nice and mostly listens and lets me talk, though every so often he stops me and asks me to think about something. So far he's asked me to think about Mom dying and whether that had any effect on what happened to me, all these years later, on the island. My seeing ghosts and so forth.

I told him that was an interesting question, because my girlfriend—my ex-girlfriend—once asked me the same thing. I'd blown up at her, but now that I was starting to feel better, I was beginning to see how that might be one theory about what happened. A few days later Dr. Lee stopped me when I was talking about my first days on the island and asked me to consider the fact that some people, especially people my age, don't do all that well with isolation and being away from home. He let me talk for another few days, and I got on the subject of Sophie, and he asked me to consider whether my breakup with Sophie might have led to some of the problems I began to have with reality.

I thought about all the things he suggested, and they all sounded reasonable to me. Very perceptive. I guess they're going to keep me here for a while. They're trying this new medication on me, and everyone seems optimistic about how well it's working.

If things go well I might get out of here in time to go back to school in the fall. I guess it will be a little weird, seeing Sophie in the halls and in my classes. But Dr. Lee has it all worked out that everyone at home will be told I had to leave Crackstone's Landing because I had a serious infection. And that part is true. I know I wrote Sophie a lot of letters about the bizarre events I imagined. But she'll understand when she finds out that I was hallucinating from fever.

She'll probably be relieved. In fact I think I'll write her and bring her up to date on my condition and apologize for everything I put her through. After all, it was her father who was nice enough to get me that job in the first place.

Also I'm glad that you got a chance to meet Linda, even if it did take me going crazy to make it happen.

I always knew you two would like each other. And I was happy to hear that you're going back to the island to see her. Maybe you two will fall in love, like I hoped. And it will all be worth it, everything that happened to me and every awful thing I went through, if it means that you and Linda could possibly get together. Not that I'm getting ahead of myself or putting any pressure on you two. But wouldn't it be funny if someday people ask you two how you met, and you say, Well, actually, we met after Linda hit my son over the head with a golf club?

I'll write you again as soon as I get a chance. Which means as soon as they let me.

Love,

Jack

EDGEWATER
AUGUST 13

DEAR SOPHIE,

As I guess you've heard, they've put me in this . . . place. Jim Crackstone is paying for it, and I think he and my dad worked out some deal where he'll pay me for all the time I spent on the island, plus compensation for getting sick. So I will have enough money for college, or maybe for a few months of college, if we're being realistic, which everyone here is always saying to do. Be realistic. Speaking of which, did you hear that my dad and Linda have sort of been seeing each other? Which is great. Maybe someday someone will think I faked this whole thing to bring my dad and Linda together.

But you'll know that I didn't. If they get together, it will probably mean that Jim Crackstone will have to hire someone beside Linda to take care of the kids. Or maybe my dad will move out there with them. I hope that doesn't happen. I can't imagine going back there, and I know my dad would never do something like that to me. Jim can find someone else. And Miles and Flora will forget Linda, like they forgot Lucy and Norris, like they'll forget me—the scary guy who tried to attack them with a golf club.

You probably know better than I do what our friends at home are saying. Supposedly, I had some infection. Which is true. But you're the only person who knows about all the other stuff.

~~Unless you already told Josh.~~

As you can see, I crossed that out. I promised Dr. Lee—my doctor here—that I would stop giving you a hard time about Josh. He says there's no evidence that you were ever cheating on me and that my thinking you did was just another sign of the hard time I was having. It was just one more thing I imagined. So I'm sorry, Sophie. I guess I put you through a lot. And you were really patient with me, trying your best to help until I couldn't be helped anymore. By you.

The doctors here are helping a lot. One theory about why I had problems was that I had too much free time and I wasn't ready to structure whole days for myself. So they've certainly taken care of that. An hour of breakfast and room cleanup, two hours of group therapy, two hours of lunch and rest, an hour of individual therapy, two hours of occupational therapy—which means covering appointment books with glitter as a present for someone we love. Do you want one? I can't exactly see giving a glitter-covered calendar to Dad, no matter how much he might appreciate the gesture.

My fellow inmates—oops, guests!—are exactly what you'd imagine if you'd seen even one film or read one book about places like this. The eating-disorder girl, the guy with the bandaged wrists, the tattooed girl who keeps freaking out and screaming because she's only allowed two cigarettes a day. I wish I could say this place is unique. But it's not. It's like someone called the casting director and said, Hey listen, send me a dozen crazies between the ages of fifteen and twenty.

But like I told you, it's helping. I understand all the reasons for what happened this summer. I also understand you were only trying to help me when you told me your theories about where my problems might be coming from. I'm sorry I was so mean.

I've come to realize that I just imagined all that stuff about the ghosts. And I guess I must have been really nervous from the beginning. Otherwise I wouldn't have had that fantasy about the seagull telling me not to go to the island. And the people I saw on the boat were definitely not Lucy and Norris, who are definitely dead.

But you know what, Sophie? One thing still confuses me.

For the first week here, they made us wear these dorky pajamas, I guess so we'd really feel like inmates or patients. I mean, guests. Then they let us put on our real clothes, after they'd searched them for pills or razor blades or whatever they imagine we might try to smuggle in. They gave me back my old jeans and T-shirt, and it felt good to look like myself again. Not that they let us have mirrors here. But I could tell I looked like me.

That first day I was at breakfast, and the tattooed girl was screaming about not being allowed to smoke. It put the rest of us on edge. I wasn't really aware of it, but I must have had my fists jammed deep in my pockets.

When I took my hands out again and opened them up, there it was.

Lucy's holy medal.

I wasn't imagining it, Sophie. I have the medal here now, with its silver frame and the image of the saint. I'm looking at it as I write. The saint of hopeless cases. And I'm praying to it. Please let me see Lucy just one more time. This time I'd tell her everything I wanted to say and didn't. But what would I say? Maybe it doesn't matter, because the saint doesn't seem to be answering my prayers.

So tell me this, Sophie. Because you always were so smart. Smarter than I ever was. Smarter than I ever will be. Tell me: If I imagined everything, the seagull and the ghosts and the morbid playing cards, if it was all just a fantasy, then where did I get this medal? And why is there still that red spot on it—that drop of Lucy's dying blood?

When I get out of here, I'll show it to you. And you can let me know what you think.

So okay, between now and then, enjoy the last

weeks of summer. Thanks for being there for me when I needed you. Thanks for reading my letters.

See you soon, I hope. If you want to see me. And I hope you do.

Meanwhile,

XOXO

Your friend,

Jack

Also from *New York Times* bestselling author
FRANCINE PROSE

★"A taut, brilliantly controlled novel."
—*Publishers Weekly*
(starred review)

"Intriguing."
—*New York Times Book Review*
California Young Reader's Medal Winner

★"Riveting."
—ALA *Booklist*
(starred review)